PUFFIN BOOKS

White Mist

Barbara Smucker is a Mennonite and lives in Waterloo, Ontario. *White Mist* reveals her concern for our environment and the Native Peoples of North America.

WHITE MIST

Barbara Smucker

PUFFIN BOOKS

PUFFIN BOOKS

Published by the Penguin Group

Penguin Books Canada Ltd., 2801 John Street, Markham,
Ontario, Canada L3R 1B4
Penguin Books, 27 Wrights Lane, London W8 5TZ, England
Viking Penguin Inc., 40 West 23rd Street,
New York, New York 10010, USA
Penguin Books Australia Ltd., Ringwood,
Victoria, Australia
Penguin Books (NZ) Ltd., 182-190 Wairau Road,
Auckland 10, New Zealand

Penguin Books Ltd., Registered Offices:
Harmondsworth, Middlesex, England

First published by Irwin Publishing Inc.
Published in Puffin Books, 1987

Reprinted 1987

Published by arrangement with Irwin Publishing Inc.

Manufactured in Canada by Gagne Printing Ltd.

Canadian Cataloguing in Publication Data

Smucker, Barbara, 1915-
   White mist

Bibliography: p.
ISBN 0-14-032144-6

I. Title.

PS8537.M82W48 1987   jC813'.54   C86-094728-9
PZ7.S6648Wh 1987

To John, my editor,
with immense gratitude

Author's Note and Acknowledgements

The characters in this book are fictitious, as is Singing Sands Beach and its pollution. The story of "buried" Singapore is true and so is the history connected with it. Chiefs Pokagon, Metea, and Menominee did exist as described in the story.

My special thanks to native people, teachers, administrators at Reserves in Moosonee, Sarnia, and Walpole Island, Ontario, Reserves in Norway House and Berens River, Manitoba, and in several public schools in Winnipeg, Manitoba; to generous librarians in Douglas and Holland, Michigan, Newton, Kansas and the University of Waterloo, Ontario; to innumerable local historians in Michigan; and to my husband, Donovan, who accompanied me on all the above journeys.

WHITE MIST

1

"Look, gang, Pocahontas is leaving school early this spring," a thin girl with a slash of blonde hair falling over one eye said loudly to her cluster of friends in the school hallway. They giggled.

"Are you going to a pow-wow, May?" another of them called.

May banged the door of her empty locker. She wanted to turn around and shout back, "Stop picking on me. What makes you think I'm an Indian? Maybe I came from Spain — or Italy — or — or Tahiti."

Instead she hunched, shy and hurt, over an armload of books and ran down the hall toward the exit.

Other times and other words trailed behind her: "Got any scalps in your locker, May?" "Ever been in a massacre?"

Not everyone in the school taunted her. The teachers didn't and she made good grades. But this gang of girls was always around and inviting others to join them. May escaped into isolation — going to the library, avoiding extra-curricular activities, going home when the final bell rang. It was no way to make friends.

Early next morning as May left her home in Sarnia, Ontario, snuggled between Aunt Nell and Uncle Steve in the front seat of their Chevy heading for summer and Lake Michigan and the Appleby Nursery, the sound of the sniping words grew dimmer. But they still rang in her ears as though the whole middle school were shouting them at her.

Why hadn't she said to the girls, "I'm leaving early because I have a summer job. The principal excused me."?

Lately in May's dreams the school had taken to rising from the earth in a rocket of giggling girls. The higher they soared, the louder they laughed.

"May, May," the rocket hissed as it headed for outer space. "You can't come along, you're different. The fat people, the crippled people, the brown people can't come along."

May squeezed closer to Uncle Steve. He smiled broadly and patted her hand. His sandy hair blew straight up in the warm breeze from the open window; his strong hand, with its freckles and blond, fuzzy hair was reassuring. Aunt Nell, ruddy-faced and plain, hummed and sang a tune about spring and the fragrance of blossoms.

That these two stocky, kindly white people were the relatives of tall, thin, black-haired, brown-skinned May was never questioned by any of them.

May loved them and they returned her love in a simple, soft-spoken way. They imagined the whole world thought she was a princess, just as they did. How could she tell them about the taunts at school and the loneliness of being "different"?

To Nell and Steve Appleby, May's arrival at their Flower Shop on the edge of Sarnia thirteen years ago was a miracle. May had heard the story over and over again.

"You were bundled in a pretty white blanket and your black hair made a shining ring around your face," Aunt Nell would say. "We found you on our doorstep."

"It was snowing and you were tucked in a box just like a Christmas present," Uncle Steve regularly added. "We had always wanted children, but had never been able to have them."

May loved hearing the story — about the note pinned to her shirt with the name May Apple printed on it; about Nell and Steve adopting her but deciding they were too old to be called Mother and Father; about not knowing and not caring if she was Indian, Spanish, Mexican, black or any combination.

The apartment above the Flower Shop near Lake Huron was their winter home and every summer the three of them left there, crossing the nearby border to work for their cousin Ardith Appleby in her Michigan nursery. In return Ardith came to Sarnia to run the Flower Shop. It was a pleasant change for them all and the Nursery needed Uncle Steve's strength for spring replanting.

Today as the Chevy whizzed over the Bluewater Bridge to Port Huron, the clear blue waters of Lake Huron sparkled on one side of the bridge, with dozens of white sailing boats looking like painted scenery. On the other side, the matching blue of the St. Clair River was busy with tugs and fishing boats.

Far in the distance May could see the smoking chimneys of Chemical Valley puffing skyward. They were not far from her school and the Flower Shop. May took a deep breath of fresh Lake air. It was good to be away from the rubbery smell of the Valley — though she knew Aunt Nell and Uncle Steve didn't agree. For them the smell meant home. Uncle Steve proudly carried a ten-dollar Canadian bill with him wherever he went, for on its back were pictured the towers, tubes, pipes and bulbous tanks of Sarnia's Chemical Valley.

He would puff out his chest and tell folks about "the largest concentration of petro-chemical complexes in the British Commonwealth".

Several hours later the ancient Chevy approached their destination, Singing Sands Beach on the western shores of Lake Michigan. May liked to think of the five Great Lakes sharing their waters where one joined another. They sped over a two-laned highway, then broke away into a smaller road with cluttered signs and ragged waste, as though the towns behind them had swept their refuse to the roadside.

At last a scattering of oaks and birches interspersed with sassafras and a few spreading sugar maples brought quiet to the landscape. Uncle Steve turned onto a sandy road that cut through the trees. At the end of it, the blue vastness of Lake Michigan stretched before them.

May caught her breath as the car stopped. She flew from the sheltering arms around her. Nearby, a rustic sign — APPLEBY NURSERY — leaned against a tree with an arrow pointing into the woodlands. Uncle Steve and Aunt Nell lifted heavy bags and headed for the building.

Singing Sands Beach! This place was May's heaven. The wide beach that ringed the shoreline was almost abandoned this early in the Spring.

"Back soon," May called to Uncle Steve and Aunt Nell, pulling off her socks and shoes.

She took a deep breath of Lake air and then whirled about toward the shaded marshland. Clusters of white trillium greeted her, and behind them in an open space were hundreds of bright, orange hawkweed. Their round, stiff blossoms seemed airborne and stemless as did the yellow buttercups beside them. Here and there were late traces of ice and snow.

Then she turned to the dampest and shadiest spot, where the dark green, umbrella-like May Apples had come up. May touched them reverently. These strange plants bore her name — the name pinned to her baby shirt. What did her real mother, or real father, mean by naming her after them?

She gently lifted the hairy, pointed leaves to find the single white blossoms beneath. She would watch them carefully and in June when they became berries would drop them into her tea and savour the special strawberry flavour.

"Watch those plants," Uncle Steve always warned her. "The leaves can be poisonous even though the berries are good." And Aunt Nell had frightened her once with a tale about them.

"They used to be called mandrakes," she said. "The roots are forked and can look like a human body. People believed that if you pulled a mandrake out of the ground, it would give out a wild shriek and everyone who heard it would go insane."

Aunt Nell had laughed over the superstition but May felt a quiver of fear.

Now she looked again at the solemn, sheltering plants. Was she imagining that a white drifting mist was circling over them? It reminded her of the ectoplasm she had seen once in a horror movie.

May jumped to her feet. Nothing could spoil her joyous return to Singing Sands. She ran off into the gently heaving water of Lake Michigan, disturbing a skittering crowd of sandpipers. Bright sunshine flecked the water in the distance with glitter on the rising edge of each small wave. Sometimes May dreamed of plunging into it and swimming unchecked all the way to Chicago. The abundance of its waters overwhelmed her.

Unexpectedly May stumbled, her feet tangling in a mass of thick green seaweed. She looked down and was startled. A school of white bellied, upturned fish rubbed against her legs. Bubbles of brown foam swished between them. A few dead fish along the beach were no surprise, but there were so many. Some of the bodies, already dried on the sand, were being pecked at by hungry gulls. Little frightened-looking fish eyes peered up at May. She tried kicking the moving ones back into deep water, but they had no will to swim or even to right themselves.

"What's happening?" she cried and backed away from the stench and debris. Now she saw that not only dead fish lined the shore; here and there also lay lifeless gulls, stretched out and stiff. Even the nervous sandpipers scuttled around them.

As May looked closer she realized that the shoreline had changed too. One of her favourite burr oak trees had fallen backward into the pines, its roots black and exposed. And much of the beach grass that held the sand dunes from sliding into the Lake was dried and brown. Already the steps that led up to the children's camp nearby were buried in sand. It looked as if in time cottages and roads and even the Appleby Nursery could slide into the Lake.

"May — Princess," Uncle Steve called loudly from the road above. "I'm driving into Saugatuck to pick up the hired man at the bus stop. Want to come along?"

May raced toward the shelter of Uncle Steve's voice. He always seemed to be on hand to rescue her — yesterday from the teasing and loneliness of her school, now from a fear that some disease had struck her beloved Lake Michigan.

''What's wrong, love?'' Uncle Steve lifted her chin and smiled into her face.

''Oh, nothing,'' May smiled back.

2

Riding beside Uncle Steve, May saw that little had changed on the road to Saugatuck. They entered the small village from the highway.

The tourists had not yet come to walk up and down the main street in their smooth white shorts and white sailing caps. But their rows of yachts and sailing boats, waiting for them in long straight docks, were in perfect order. The shops were bright with new paint and some of the window boxes were already filled with blooming red geraniums. Uncle Steve and May parked near the bus stop, which was just a plain bench on the sidewalk with a Greyhound Bus sign painted above it.

"Might as well walk down the street while we're waiting." Uncle Steve swung open the car door for May. It was comfortable strolling by the quaint shops and sidewalk restaurants.

"This is my favourite small town," May confided.

"Mine too," Uncle Steve grinned and took hold of her hand.

They stopped at the white, freshly painted city hall. Uncle Steve walked inside but May lingered near the historic marker that stood in front of it. She felt a weird tugging at her feet as though a magnet was holding them fast to the sidewalk. Maybe she had stepped on fresh cement or a wad of chewing gum? She slid her shoes back and forth: the cement was smooth and clean. It was strange — and a little scary.

May began to read the sign. The story it told always fascinated her. It added a special mystery to this small town that stood trim and neat behind the high wooded sand dunes, straddling the wide, slow-moving Kalamazoo River whose mouth emptied into the giant Lake.

May read it quickly.

Beneath the sands near the mouth of the Kalamazoo River lies the site of Singapore, one of Michigan's most famous ghost towns. Founded in the 1830's by New York speculators, who hoped it would rival Chicago or Milwaukee as a lake port, Singapore was in fact, until the 1870's, a busy lumbering town — with three mills, two hotels, several general stores, and a renowned "Wild Cat" bank. . . . When the supply of timber was exhausted the mills closed, the once bustling waterfront grew quiet. The people left . . . . Gradually, Lake Michigan's shifting sand buried Singapore.

As May came to the last line, the letters on the marker began to shake and then blur. They were covered with the same white, drifting mist that had floated in and out of the May Apples on the beach. A small breeze from the Lake blew up suddenly and began whipping around her. The marker and the buildings of Saugatuck slowly faded and May found that she was standing alone. But only for an instant, for in front of her the tall, stately figure of an Indian slowly emerged.

He was a chief, May was certain. His soft white hair hung to his shoulders and his troubled, intelligent eyes stared straight into hers. On his head was a brightly decorated animal-skin turban with something that looked like a human rib-bone protruding from the top of it. A buckskin cloak swung about his shoulders.

The breeze now swirled strongly around the two of them. There were no words spoken and May felt no fear; only sadness and a growing warmth and kinship for this dignified man.

The wind stopped as quickly as it had come and the silent Indian chief somehow evaporated with it. May was certain she had seen him, and she was just as certain that Uncle Steve had not. He was now walking out of the city hall building.

I can't tell him, May decided quickly. He would worry and how could I explain it to him?

"I've got bad news, Princess." Uncle Steve frowned, obviously unaware of the sudden wind and the appearance of a stranger on the street. His ruddy, weather-beaten face sagged under the eyes and his usual kindly smile had disappeared into tight-lipped disapproval. But May was too shaken by the visitation of the Indian to be concerned.

Uncle Steve grabbed May's hand and they started back toward the bus stop bench.

"They say there's so much pollution in the Lake that swimming won't be allowed on Singing Sands Beach until it's cleaned up," Uncle Steve said grimly. "Some of the fish are poisoned and can't be eaten."

May was alarmed. "This has never happened before," she said.

"Well, don't you worry too much, Princess," said Uncle Steve. "The town authorities are investigating and are calling in help from the state environmental agencies."

They sat down together on the long bench and Uncle Steve started leafing through some papers he had pulled from his pocket.

"Seems like the hired hand Ardith employed for the summer comes from Sarnia too," he muttered to himself. "Name is Lee Pokagon — sixteen — didn't finish high school, worked last summer picking blueberries in this area — good recommendations from his employers."

May was not too interested. She had more important things to think about. It was interesting, however, that he came from Sarnia.

The blue-streaked bus swung around the corner and slowed to a stop in front of them. The door opened and only one passenger stepped out. He was a lanky, thin-waisted young man with long black hair tied at the back in a pony tail. His skin was brown, the same shade as May's. A leather-beaded headband circled his head and he wore a buckskin jacket with a fringe around the bottom.

When he turned to face them, May jumped to her feet in amazement. He had the same look and expression as the Indian chief who had stood in front of her minutes before. Only this man was young and his hair was black instead of flowing white.

3

May was confused and frightened. Could her imagination really have created a ghost-like image to appear beside the Singapore sign? Was she so obsessed with Indians that she thought the new summer helper resembled the Indian chief?

Of course not, she scolded herself. She would handle this whole incident with some of Aunt Nell's "good sense". Lee Pokagon just happened to be an Indian who came from Sarnia. There was a Chippewa Reserve next to Chemical Valley and not far from their Flower Shop. He probably lived there. He would work all summer with Uncle Steve and she would probably see very little of him. She would think of some sensible explanation for the Indian chief later.

And besides, more important to her now was the sickness of her beloved Lake Michigan. Not to be able to plunge in each day for a long swim to the sand bar would destroy the joy of summer. When she stretched herself fully into the current and let the pounding waves lift her floating onto the surface of the Lake, May was at peace. The Lake was her kin, her special bond with Mother Nature.

May's thoughts were disturbed abruptly when Lee opened the car door to let her step into the back. She was surprised. No one had been this polite to her before. He slid into the front seat near Steve.

They were total opposites, May noticed. Lee was as

tall and straight as a flag pole with his thick, black pony tail announcing his identity. Uncle Steve, slumped and round-shouldered under his faded checked shirt, was a hard-working lovable beaver with no concern at all for his appearance. But he did like to talk and seemed unaware that Lee hadn't yet said one word.

"Five hundred roses arrived this morning from the polyhouse," he was saying to Lee, ". . .those plastic covered houses where they were protected all winter. You and May will have to get them into the soil and pots right away."

Lee leaned forward with interest, then turned and stared at May. There was a fleeting glance of recognition between them, May was certain, and she was startled. He *did* resemble the Indian chief!

"You must be May Apple," he said excitedly. Then he turned back to Uncle Steve.

A shiver spread through May. Her body seemed filled with prickling needles. How did this young Indian know her name? She was positive that she had never seen him before and had never heard his name.

Evidently Uncle Steve hadn't noticed.

"If you've never potted roses before, Lee," Uncle Steve went on, unaware of May's turmoil, "May can show you. She's better at it than I am."

May was embarrassed now as well as confused and frightened. But she was also a little pleased. She had never thought before that her knowledge and care of plants and trees was any special achievement.

Uncle Steve hunched over the steering wheel.

"Nell and I will be as busy as bees getting all the evergreens out into the sales area before the customers begin to arrive."

The car rounded a bend on the sandy road, drawing closer to Lake Michigan and the Appleby Nursery. A surprise wind blew off the water carrying a putrid smell.

"That smells like dead fish," Lee said with alarm. "The Lake must be polluted."

Uncle Steve was flustered. His easy-going nature didn't fit with unexpected disasters, especially when his own hard work couldn't bring about a remedy.

"It is," he fussed, parking the car close to a low, log-framed building with baskets of red petunias swinging from an overhanging entrance beam. APPLEBY NURSERY was carved in scrolled letters above a wide door. "But the smell won't last long. The authorities will clean it up."

"This can't happen to Lake Michigan." Lee seemed troubled and May was impressed by the determination in his voice.

Aunt Nell bounded through the door, her large legs cased in worn blue jeans as tight as skin. Her faded green flannel garden shirt hung comfortably around her large body like a tent and a smudge of dirt streaked one cheek. She greeted them heartily, with a full smile.

"Welcome to Appleby's," she cried, grabbing the hesitant Lee by the hand and pulling him swiftly into the nursery building. She surveyed him quickly.

"So you don't have a bag." The pony tail and beaded headband were seemingly unnoticed. May speculated that she must have already known he was an Indian.

Aunt Nell continued loudly, "The only clothes you've got are the ones on your back, I'll bet." She led him toward a door at the back of the shop and swung it open, revealing a neatly made bed, small dresser, desk and chair. An array of work clothes hung on the wall.

"Get yourself tidied up," Nell ordered. "No need to wear your best clothes. Put on one of those work outfits, then we'll have some late lunch and get to work."

Uncle Steve jokingly called his wife "the General" when she ordered people around. May, Steve and Nell gathered in Ardith's living quarters on the opposite side of the Nursery from Lee's room and the three of them prepared lunch together.

"Did you hear about the pollution in the Lake, Nell?" Steve looked sideways at his wife as he cut thick slices from a loaf of bread.

Nell laughed. "Nobody can pollute a Lake as big as Michigan. One big storm and whatever problem there is along the shore will wash away. Just mark my word." She laughed again and poured pink lemonade into tall, plastic glasses.

"Do you really think so, Aunt Nell?" May asked, wanting desperately to believe her.

When Lee appeared, unsmiling and silent, May decided that even in patched and worn work clothes he had the trim walk and proud appearance of someone important — as important as the Indian chief. She liked the way he looked. Then she stiffened. The thin white mist that had hovered over the May Apples near the beach this morning was drifting like frail threads about Lee's head. She wasn't imagining it, for Lee saw it too. He lifted his hand to brush it away.

"There's smoke blowing around my head," he said.

"Smoke?" Aunt Nell laughed. "You're dizzy from the bus ride, Lee. If there's smoke in here it's inside your head. Now let's eat."

The mist drifted away.

"You two will work in the potting shed." Nell nodded toward May and Lee. "Might as well get started right away." As soon as they had finished eating she shooed them outside toward a small lean-to. When they got there and were finally alone May forgot her usual shyness.

"It's best not to hurry potting rose plants," she told Lee, wanting to help him. "That's why I'm better at this job than Aunt Nell. She gets impatient."

She was amazed that she could talk so easily to a stranger. But was Lee a stranger? Hadn't he recognized her in the car? And he did know her name.

"She's not really your aunt, is she, May?" Lee looked amused.

"Of course she's my aunt!" May said defensively.

"Who do you think you're kidding? You're an Indian too, May, just like me," Lee said angrily. "There's no way you can hide it."

May's defences crumpled. She could never talk back and defend herself. Her usual shyness swept over her like a protective blanket.

"I don't know who I am. I really don't," she mumbled, wishing she could run away from Lee's strange probing.

Lee was puzzled. "What do you mean you don't know who you are?"

Without warning, a dam seemed to break inside May. The whole story of her adoption spilled out in a flood. Never before had she told anyone about the baby on the doorstep of the flower shop in Sarnia. She had always just listened to Uncle Steve and Aunt Nell and held back her questions and resentments.

"It was a miracle, just as they said." May looked up from her potting directly at Lee. "They did adopt me and I belong to them and I love them. I couldn't love them more even if we all had black hair, brown eyes and dark skin." May couldn't believe that she was talking so openly. She began potting one rose plant after another with nervous speed. Lee joined her and was silent.

"And what about my real mother and real father?" May's voice rose. "Why did they put me in a box and give me away? Why didn't they tell somebody where I came from and why — why I was different?" She wiped tears from her eyes. "All they gave me was a name — May Apple."

Lee looked up instantly, dropping his dirt-filled pot and spilling the sifted black soil in all directions. He stared at May and then said quietly,

"Your mother and father gave you an important gift, May. There's something very special about your name. I knew it the minute your uncle called you May in the car coming back from the bus stop."

Uncle Steve entered the room covered with peat moss and green needles from some newly balled white pines. He frowned at the spilled dirt covering the floor. He was neat about the Nursery grounds and buildings even though his clothes were usually dishevelled. He did seem pleased, however, with the potted roses.

"The General has ordered an end to the work day." He smiled. "She's serving a bowl of stew to all of us as soon as we wash our hands. Then an early bed and up at sunrise."

4

In the brisk, sunny days that followed, May and Lee worked constantly together. Aunt Nell declared that Lee consumed information about the Nursery ''in gulps''. He asked May details about every plant, flower and tree. Several times she tried to divert him and ask how he had guessed her name. He shrugged off her question and didn't reply.

Only once did he talk about his home on the Sarnia Reserve. It was on a day when a customer came to the Nursery and said to Uncle Steve,

''When did you get your Indian helper, Steve? Aren't you afraid the boy will become careless and run away? You know about 'lazy Indians'.''

Lee heard him from a back room and stamped outside to the potting shed. May followed.

''Uncle Steve doesn't think that,'' she said quickly. ''He says you're the best summer help he's ever had.''

May was worried. She realized that Lee really might leave if he thought there was prejudice toward him in the area. She knew how he felt. Hadn't she often wanted to run away from her school for the same reason?

But she wanted Lee to stay. Having him here filled a great lonely place inside her. It wasn't that Uncle Steve and Aunt Nell weren't friends and companions. May quickly admitted their care and goodness. But she always felt she must protect them from her fears, resentments and even loneliness. How could she protest against their kindness? How could she explain the importance of the difference in their ages?

With Lee it was different. She could say anything in front of him. She could blurt out angrily, "I still don't think I'm an Indian, even though you keep telling me I look like one."

Sometimes Lee laughed, sometimes he scolded, but often he withdrew in angry silence.

Today in the potting shed, he wanted to talk, though his voice was surly.

"There are lots of reasons why I came here to work this summer. I can't tell you yet about the main one — but I can tell you that I think I deserve this job." He shifted his feet impatiently. "I worked hard last summer on those blueberries and I'm good with trees and plants and even flowers. It's all legal too. A relative around here got me a work permit to come."

"You don't have to prove all that to me," May snapped. "I believe you and so does Uncle Steve. Who cares what one stupid customer says?"

"Well, I care." There was bitterness now and a briefly exposed fear. "One of the reasons I left the reserve this time was because my cousin Joe committed suicide." Lee kicked the wall of the shed.

May felt her heart freeze. Lee stared at the floor.

"He was my best friend. We went hunting and skiing and played bingo together and we quit school on the same day. . . . He didn't tell me he was going to do it. He didn't say anything. . . . They flew the flag at half-mast on the reserve the day it happened."

May wanted to help, but she couldn't speak. Her voice was as frozen as her heart.

"They said Joe was an alcoholic just like my Dad." Hurt and pain were in Lee's words. "He lost a job

because of it — and then his girl-friend. . . I miss him.
He told stories that made me laugh."

"I'm sorry, Lee."

Lee blew his nose loudly into a dirty red bandana and
stuffed it into his pocket.

"That man who came in here needs a kick in the
teeth." Lee shook one of the pots on the shelf until the
plant stem broke.

They never talked about Joe again.

The topic that consumed them most of the time —
even Aunt Nell — was the continuing pollution at
Singing Sands Beach. The dead fish did not go away.
They slurped onto the broad sandy shore day after day.
Wide-toothed shovels scooped them into trucks that
dumped them at a fertilizer plant. But the putrid smell
lingered like a disease that could not be cured just by
hiding the patient in isolation.

Vacationers came to open their summer cottages and
in less than a day closed the shutters or pulled down the
blinds and drove away. Appleby's Nursery was threatened since it depended on the summer customers. The
Nursery was bursting with new plants and trees
needing to be planted.

"It's still early in the season," Aunt Nell maintained.
"When the hot weather comes, our beach will be back
to normal."

May no longer believed her.

An ugly NO SWIMMING sign remained mounted on
a post in the centre of the beach. One morning as May
and Lee inspected the Lake they stopped in horror. The
filmy white mist, that to May looked like ectoplasm,
was looping itself around the sign. It was thicker and
was guiding its own movements, and did not just blow
away with the wind.

"It's the same stuff that swirled around my head the day I came." Lee was awed. He walked toward it to grab hold. When he lifted his hand the substance vanished.

Neither of them spoke for a while. May was unsettled. But a few moments later she surprised herself by saying, "I hope you come back again next summer, Lee."

Lee looked at her intently with a peculiar, quizzical expression.

"I have to keep coming to this place," he said almost in a whisper. "I've been wanting to tell you about the day last summer when I walked into Saugatuck. I was standing in front of the big historical marker near the city hall when. . ."

He didn't finish because Uncle Steve burst breathlessly into their conversation.

5

"We've got a rush order from one of the yacht builders down near the mouth of the Kalamazoo," Uncle Steve panted, brushing pine needles from his rumpled hair. "He wants a dozen white pines at once. We're to deliver them and plant them."

May wasn't listening. What had Lee wanted to tell her about his experience at city hall. Had he also seen the Indian chief?

"May — Princess." Uncle Steve shook her to attention. "Nell and I can't leave the shop now. You and Lee will have to do this job. You've got a driver's license, Lee. Can you handle a motor boat?"

May sighed. There were always crises at the nursery in early spring.

"We'd better take the trees to the Lake in the pick-up truck," she said, "and then haul them by motor boat up the river."

"I can take care of the truck and the motor boat and May can give me directions." Lee tightened the belt of his patched jeans around his waist.

Within half an hour the small, newly balled pines were in the truck and May and Lee were driving off.

"Be careful," Aunt Nell shouted after them. "I'll have dinner ready at 6:00."

Soon they were back at the Lake's edge where the motor boat was moored. The stench of dying fish was everywhere. Lee frowned. Here and there people were raking the fish into piles. A scoop shovel was digging deep holes in the sand and lifting them in. Others were being dumped into the back of a heavy truck. Some of the Lake water around them had become trapped in slime and May pushed her boat away from it before stepping inside.

"Better stay near the shore," May called out to Lee as he started the motor. She pointed east toward the harbour. It was odd: there were no other boats in sight and, except for the rakers, the scoop shovel and the truck, the beaches, as far as May could see, were empty. The debris-filled water sickened her.

As they pushed into the water it looked to May as though the Lake and the shoreline were out of focus. A fuzzy backdrop of tall pine trees seemed to hover behind the shore and above them was the thin, wispy white substance that had circled the NO SWIMMING sign. A shiver ran through May. Lee's attention was focussed on the motor boat.

It was a short trip and they soon entered the mouth of the Kalamazoo through the wide harbour and anchored at the nearest wharf. May looked up nervously toward the tall pines, but the hovering mist had disappeared.

In front of them was a sweeping yellow beach where a low-built home was tucked behind scattered oak and cedars. An elderly man with furrowed lines pinched tightly between his eyes met them at the dock. He supported himself with a pine cane carved in the likeness of a snake. The open-mouthed head curved downward into a handle. May was positive that she saw the head move and the jaws snap open.

"Glad to see you so prompt with the trees." His voice cracked slightly with age. "I want them lined up straight in front of the house." He swung his cane upward. "If Singing Sands Beach is going to be polluted,

I don't want to see it. You'll find white stakes where each tree should go.'' He shuffled slowly away toward some elderly fishermen crouched along the river bank nearby.

"Looks like Appleby's hired some Indians for the summer,'' one of them commented.

"He's in for a lot of trouble, then,'' another one warned.

May's stomach tightened. They weren't just talking about Lee. They meant her too.

Lee's face became a mask, immovable and expressionless. Silently the two of them moved shovels and trees to the row of stakes. Lee's strength astonished May. A row of deep holes was dug swiftly and the trees planted and watered. Lee finally broke the silence.

"It's good to plant trees, even in the wrong places.''

"I'm sorry about more Indian talk, Lee.'' May couldn't avoid mentioning it. "It makes me sick. I don't even know if I am one.''

Lee pushed his shovel deep into the yellow sand.

"What's wrong, May? Afraid to face who you are?'' The shadow of a smile broke through his mask. "My own feeling is that you were born on the Sarnia Reserve.''

May started to protest. Then shrugged her shoulders. It was possible, she had to admit. Then she remembered the taunting girls at school who sniffed whenever they mentioned the Reserve. "It's poor and run down,'' one of them had scoffed. "The chemical plants should take it over.''

"I get sick of the oil smells around there sometimes, don't you?'' May had said finally.

They finished the tree planting far ahead of schedule and began to walk upstream along the Kalamazoo.

When they sat on an old pier to rest, the fishermen along the river focussed on them like sentries.

"Funny thing," Lee said, stretching his long legs over the sand, "I always pretended that I was a white guy when I went to school. I'd never say to the kids that I was an Indian. I didn't want anybody to know that my Dad was a drunk and didn't live at home much."

"Drunken Indian," May murmured softly.

"Yeah," Lee shrugged. "You hear it all the time. It gives you an inferiority complex. You'd think all of us were drunk all the time."

May agreed. That's what she had at school all right — an inferiority complex. She ran her hand over the pier.

"Have you read that historical marker in Saugatuck, Lee, about the buried city of Singapore?"

"Lots of times," he answered.

May hoped he would finish telling about his trip to the city hall that he'd mentioned earlier. It seemed best to let him bring it up.

"Isn't this where Singapore is, right here underneath us?" May's voice sounded far away. Another unexpected cool breeze started circling around them. The old fishermen pulled their coat collars up. "I guess all that's left of Singapore today are these barren sand dunes and those rotten pilings over there." May had to shout for the breeze had turned into a swishing wind.

"This old pier we're sitting on must have been there too," Lee shouted back to her.

But to May the pier no longer looked so old. It had become smooth and sturdy. Had it changed this way for Lee too?

Across the river directly ahead of them, the wind was not blowing and Mount Baldhead, the highest sand dune in the area with its green undergrowth and sandy crown, stood out like a painting. A thin thread of smoke rose skyward from its peak. Or was it the same substance that had been floating near them for the past couple of weeks?

"Listen, May." Lee was tense.

The sound of drums — Indian drums — rose with the smoke. Then a high, thin, reed-like voice wailed forth with the rhythm. Whoops and yells erupted like volcanoes.

"It's the Potawatomi spring feast of Thanksgiving," Lee murmured as though in a trance. "They are celebrating the end of winter and the coming of new life from the Great Spirit who has brought back the sun."

"But, Lee, I've come here every spring for many years." May said with awe. "I've never heard them before. And look, those old fishermen can't hear the celebration at all. They're bent over fishing."

Lee continued, paying no attention to May:

"They have sailed down the Lake in canoes from their winter hunting on the Straits. Soon they will set up farms and villages along the water for the summer."

"They can't set up temporary homes, Lee. There are cottages all along the water," May protested. She hugged her sweat shirt around her. "It's getting so cold."

The noises from the celebration on Mount Baldhead continued. May realized that Lee wasn't listening to her. His eyes had become distant and unfamiliar. He looked over and through her but not at her. He was seeing something in the distance that was completely blocked from her vision.

"I'll make some tea to warm us," he said finally.

He gathered twigs and logs into a deep hollow of sand and struck a match to them. From a knapsack on his back which May hadn't noticed before, he took a pan, a thermos of water, two tin cups and a handful of dried sassafras bark.

"Go over to that marshy place, May, and pick a May Apple blossom. It will flavour our tea," Lee called out above the rising wind.

6

The beat of the drums from nearby Mount Baldhead grew louder, stirring in May a powerful response to the ancient rhythm. It pounded through her flesh against her bones and carried her in thought to times of tribal warfare and distant hunting grounds that knew no settled pioneers. Abruptly the rhythmic singing changed to raucous yells and shouts.

"The white man's firewater." Lee was enraged. "It turns the celebration into a big joke for those who drink it. It drives them wild." Lee's face became expressionless again.

"How do you know so much about all this?" May stood up straight with arms akimbo, the strong, cool wind whipping her black hair back into sheets of raven wings. For the first time in her life she felt defiant and on an equal footing with this lanky young Indian boy kneeling on the sand stirring a steaming brew of tea.

"I studied all winter at the Reserve library about the Potawatomi. That's the name of our tribe, May."

"What do you mean, our tribe!" May shouted, partly to be heard above the wind and partly because she was frightened and angry. Flying sand stung her eyes and peppered her skin. "I don't belong to a tribe and I don't even think I'm an Indian."

Lee's expression didn't change.

"You better pick the May Apple blossom. It gives just the right flavour to the sassafras."

May obeyed even though she thought it was the fruit and not the blossom that flavoured tea. She was shivering and the tea would warm her.

Lee dropped part of the blossom into her cup and the other part into his.

May held the warm cup eagerly in her hands and sipped the hot red brew. The faint strawberry aroma of May Apple blossom seeped dreamily about her. There was numbing deliciousness in the taste. She no longer felt angry with Lee or puzzled by the drum-beating and Lee's weird behaviour.

But the tea soon became difficult to drink. It started swirling around away from her lips. She looked at Lee. His tea was doing the same thing. Then, slowly, the cup began to grow to accommodate the swirling. May tried to grab it, but the cup grew larger and larger as the spinning continued, until it was no longer a cup but an expanding hole in the sand. There was no way to drink or hold it now.

The hole became a whirlwind, spinning the sand in a circle around May and Lee and blotting out the beach, the river, the fishermen and the bright afternoon sun.

May grabbed Lee's hand. She tried to shout but her voice spun into a whine. "We're being sucked down into the sand, Lee. Don't let go. Hang onto me!"

Without warning the tiny gable of a house poked above the sand in front of them. The swirling lessened. May's words began to come together. More of the house beneath the gable appeared. It was a stark, gray unpainted wooden structure. The sand continued to swish away, revealing several floors, a brick-walled basement and a wide porch, reached by a stairway as steep as a cliff.

As though exhausted, the sand finally settled silently on the beach around the house and the calmed air became still, crisp and cool.

"Of course," May said to Lee, "it's early spring. Some of the snow in Saugatuck hasn't melted yet." She stopped, amazed by what she had just said.

"Lee." May was trembling. "I don't understand this, but I think we have come down through the sand. I think we are in the buried city of Singapore."

Lee was not listening. Watching his startled expression, May thought of a child perched at the top of a cascading waterfall. She reached for Lee's hand to steady herself, for the spinning all around her had made her dizzy, even though she and Lee had stood perfectly still since drinking the tea. Lee's eyes were wary.

"I can't believe this has happened, May, but I think I should tell you something." Lee's voice was unsteady and breathless. "One day last summer when I was standing in front of the city hall in Saugatuck, reading the sign about buried Singapore, a tall Indian chief with long white hair appeared in front of me. He was wearing a bone that looked like a human rib in his headdress. I couldn't speak. I just looked at him."

A chill ran down May's back.

"Then he said to me in English with a strange accent, 'You will come to me with the help of May Apple. You will meet her in Saugatuck. Tea, brewed from the plant of her name, will bring you to me.' I didn't see him again, but I thought about him all winter. That's why I studied the Potawatomi Indians and that's why I wanted to come back here this summer."

"I saw him too." May's voice was also breathless. "In front of the city hall just before your bus pulled in. My name really does have something to do with our being here, because we drank May Apple blossom in our tea!''

A shrill squealing cry cut through the crisp air, ending their conversation. It was followed by another shriek and then another.

Before them, shining in the afternoon sun, were golden piles of lumber stacked around a makeshift building. From a tall chimney towering above it, rose an arrow of white smoke that puffed into the sky. It looked like that strange, filmy mist again.

''A sawmill, of course!'' Lee cried.

Sweating men in thick, plaid coats sloshed along the shore and in and out of the mill in heavy boots that scarred the beach into a muddy mixture of sand and sawdust. Piles of sawdust seeped like yellow ribbons into the water.

Some of the men reached out to floating logs with sturdy poles fitted at the end with spikes. They pulled the logs one by one up to the chain that fed them into the saw. Then the screeching saws took possession of them, slicing them one by one into stacks of smooth lumber.

May and Lee hid behind a large oak tree near the sprawling gray house.

''Our blue jeans and sweat shirts will single us out at once as strangers,'' Lee whispered. May's shirt was green and Lee's a brilliant blue.

An attractive, sturdy woman dressed in a long full skirt with a tight-fitting gray blouse buttoned high around her neck stepped onto the porch of the house. Her hair was pulled straight back from her face into a tight bun.

''It's the Singapore Boarding House, Lee.'' May was excited. ''I read about it in Uncle Steve's books on local history. It had apartments, a big kitchen and a dining room where lots of the mill workers ate. But, Lee, that was at least a hundred and fifty years ago!''

Lee's attention was drawn to the wharf where tugs, flat boats and schooners with furled sails were being loaded with lumber. One of the schooners had ''Chicago'' printed along its side.

The air in the town was electric with danger and busy excitement. The lumbermen were caught up in a frenzy of work. No one idled along the beach for a sun bath; no one napped on the river bank over a fishing rod.

''What's the terrible hurry all about, Lee?'' May was still clutching his hand. ''It's as if they can't wait to pull in one log after another.''

Lee looked pale. ''Don't forget, May, these are pioneer times. White settlers are pouring in by the hundreds. They need lumber for homes, boarding houses, warehouses, boats, ships, buildings in Chicago, Detroit and Sarnia. Most of them don't know and don't care that just a short time ago Michigan and Ontario belonged to the Indians. Each of these logs, May, shovels money into the pockets of the sawmill owners.''

''Let's walk up the river and get away from this noise.'' May's head was beginning to ache.

Lee agreed. ''With all these people around, somebody is going to notice us. Then I don't know what we will do.''

It was easy to slip behind trees and shrubs away from the buildings and people of bustling Singapore. As they walked through the underbrush they stepped into small piles of snow. Only a few logs were floating in the upper river because chunks of ice still jammed its flow.

''In another few weeks all the ice will melt and the logs will really start to roll.'' Lee pointed to the opposite bank where hundreds of logs were piled waiting to be released into the flowing Kalamazoo.

May looked along the high dunes, still covered with luxuriant white pines. Their massive trunks were lofty and straight and the lower branches spread out higher than the tallest man's upward reach. The pine smell from the trees and from the dripping sap at the lumber mill was pungent and delicious.

"These must be the white pine forests that were totally cut down," May said almost reverently. "Uncle Steve told me about them. These trees have been here for centuries — thousands of them. Look, Lee, the lower branches are so high, it's like a cathedral underneath — cool and shady and hidden from the sun. White pines like these don't reseed easily."

"The tallest ones must be at least a hundred feet high." Lee looked skyward. The tossing long pine needles swept elegantly across the sky. This virgin forest was a dominion of kings and queens — a truly royal forest.

May and Lee were so shaken and amazed by their entrance into buried Singapore that they had forgotten the beating drums that had seemed to shake the sand dunes across the river from the home of the old man with the snake-carved cane. The drums were silent now and the cries and shouting had ceased, for the Potawatomi celebration of Thanksgiving had come to an end. Men, women and children stalked single file without a sound down the steep dune to their waiting birchbark canoes anchored along the river bank. The boats, carefully packed with blankets, guns, fishing tackle and supplies of dried corn and pemmican, were ready to sail.

From their hiding place on the opposite shore, Lee had been the first to notice the long, narrow canoes with their slender masts. He was so excited that he grabbed May's hand and pointed toward them.

"Our people, May," he said, "are leaving Mount Baldhead and going down the river to Lake Michigan to set up summer villages along the shore. I've studied these boats. They're called Mackinaws." Lee hurried to the shore to get a better look and pulled May along with him. "They were probably the best boats in the world at the time for combining size and lightness. See, May, they're made of great strips of birchbark stretched over ribs of cedar and sewn together with cords of deerskin. Black pitch along the seams keeps the water out."

May wondered if they should expose themselves like this. Wouldn't it be safer away from the river? They were so close now that she could see the Indian people in the boats. All of them wore deerskin clothes and the girls her age had long black braids hanging down their backs. Their hair, held back with beaded bands, glistened beautifully in the sunlight.

Most of the canoes carried whole families of at least ten people. In the one closest to them, a man with a single eagle feather protruding from his animal-hide turban sat at the stern steering downriver. Two women did the hard work of paddling. In between them were children, alert and quiet, sitting among the equipment and supplies.

Cloth sails were unfurled from the cedar masts and soon there was a handsome procession of Mackinaw canoes sailing down the Kalamazoo.

Lee raced to the edge of the shore, waving with both hands. May was alarmed. What was wrong with him? Did he want to be captured? She broke away and ran into the bush. How could he welcome people he didn't know, especially people from another century?

Lee's frantic waving immediately caught the attention of a tall Indian man who sat in the stern of the largest boat which sailed with dignity and precision at the head of the procession. The man changed its course and headed toward Lee.

May was shocked and drew back even farther into the shadows, but she continued to watch.

As the boat came closer to Lee, the man stood up, grabbed Lee's hand and pulled him quickly into the boat. Lee looked back frantically, searching for May. But May could not move. She could not utter a sound. The boat pulled away from the shore and headed for Lake Michigan.

May's heart beat wildly. Lee was gone. She could not reach him now even if she ran down to the river. She was alone in "buried" Singapore — and the man who had drawn Lee into the boat had long white hair with a human rib bone stuck through his turban. He was the Indian chief May had seen beside the city hall in Saugatuck.

7

May panicked. For the first time in her life she didn't have Aunt Nell and Uncle Steve nearby to help. This aloneness was like falling into an empty cavern with no exits for escape. Besides she was trapped in another time. If only this could be some witch-filled nightmare that would blessedly evaporate with waking up. But it was not. The procession of Indian canoes, with Lee in one of them, was so far downriver from her now that the boats were only small black dots on the blue water.

May felt that she could not move from the protecting shrubs around her. Her panic was turning to despair when she looked down and saw a soft, timid baby rabbit hopping onto her shoe. Impulsively she bent to pick it up, but the tiny, frightened creature scuttled into the bushes.

"That's me," May said aloud. "Frightened, timid, shy May Appleby." She stamped her foot. Then, looking down, discovered she had smashed the green umbrella leaves of a May Apple plant.

"Will it scream?" she wondered, remembering Aunt Nell's grisly story about the roots resembling human bodies. She leaned down to straighten the twisted leaves and was surprised.

Touching them was like clasping a reassuring hand. She suddenly had compassionate thoughts toward her real mother and father who must have given her the plant's name. May Apples with their single white hidden blossom had lived for centuries, May thought. Somehow their dark green hairy-looking leaves were a living connection for her with the far past, the immediate past in Saugatuck and her strange experiences at the moment in Singapore.

Months ago, after Aunt Nell's frightening tale about their roots, May had looked up the plant in a musty old book on herbs. She remembered that its golden berries, as well as flavouring tea, could put one to sleep . . . that in the Middle Ages the mandrake was part of the concoction dropped into a witch's cauldron and that magicians used it to cast spells . . . . and that North American Indians knew the virtues of its roots as a healing medicine after extracting poison.

The Indians! In her mind May could see clearly the shadowy, white-haired Indian chief beside Saugatuck's city hall with the human rib bone protruding from his headpiece. Now this same chief was sailing down the river with Lee in his canoe.

May was certain that he had intended them to come to him in buried Singapore together.

"If only I hadn't been so scared," May murmured. She longed to be in the canoe with Lee.

With new determination, May decided that she could not hide like a timid rabbit. She would follow the river back to Singapore, walk up the stairs of the large, gray Boarding House and talk with its owner. She would ask where the Indians had their summer village and somehow she would make her way there and join Lee.

There was no time to be afraid. May decided to follow an open path along the river's edge. It was nipping cold and frozen patches of snow on the ground made hurried walking risky. The walls of cut logs lined along the top of the dunes cast unnatural box-like shadows on the river water. For thousands of years before the loggers had come, May thought, the only shadows on the Kalamazoo River had been the swaying branches of virgin pine.

Two white-tailed deer, across the river from May, drank peacefully from the clean, sparkling water. Flashes of jumping fish appeared here and there like airplane wings against the sun. Airplane wings? May laughed. Singapore had never seen a plane.

The flashing water near her looked clean enough for her to drink for no logs had yet tumbled in to disturb it. May remembered Uncle Steve talking about how it must have been ''in the good old Singapore days''. She cupped her hands excitedly, filled them with water and took a long, delicious drink. A quick memory of her own polluted Singing Sands Beach momentarily nauseated her.

As she bent over, her foot slipped into the water and her shoe filled with sand. She sat down to empty it and heard a rustling noise behind her. Turning around May saw a young white woman in a long, full skirt and tied-back blondeish hair, walking to the water with a pail. She jogged a plump baby on one hip.

''I'll fill the pail with water for you,'' May called out, without thinking where she was or who the woman might be.

The woman halted and stared at May. Her wide blue eyes were both pleased and puzzled but not afraid. The baby also stared. His face was a duplicate of his mother's — blonde hair and astonished blue eyes.

''You speak English — oh, you speak English!'' The girl rushed to May and grabbed her hand. ''I can't imagine who you are with your Indian face and black hair and your strange looking boy's clothes.'' She scanned May critically. ''But you are a girl and you speak my language!''

May was pleased too. The young mother had to be older than she, but not too much. She resembled, somewhat, the blonde girl at the Sarnia school who harassed her so much. Maybe her offer to help this woman had broken down any hostility between them. The girl sat her fat baby on the sandy beach.

"My name is Emily Morrison. I've been alone for weeks because my husband is a trader with the Indians. He had to go to Boston for new supplies."

"Oh," May exclaimed trying quickly to adjust to nineteenth-century life.

"You can't imagine what it's like," Emily Morrison sighed. "There's no one to talk with but baby Jonathan here who only laughs and cries. Bless him. And then there are the Indians who come night after night and only know one or two words in English."

"You're very brave," May said impulsively, trying to imagine herself alone in the same predicament.

"Brave?" the girl laughed. "I've so much to do there isn't time to be afraid. There's fresh water to haul each day. We have a cow to milk and chickens to tend and I'm starting a garden." She handed May the pail.

"Do you want me to carry the water to your home for you?" May didn't want to leave this friendly, talkative girl.

"Oh would you?" Emily's eyes filled with tears. "I could use some help, I really could." She paused and asked abruptly. "You don't need a job, do you? I can only give you board and room."

"Yes I do." May was surprised at her prompt reply. She began to justify it quickly. This girl had mentioned seeing Indians every night. She would probably give her just as much information about the summer villages as the manager of the Singapore Boarding House. She needed May's help and she was friendly.

''I haven't even asked your name or where you come from,'' Emily laughed again.

''It's May Appleby,'' May answered simply. ''I've come from a — a distant place in Canada with my — my friend to visit Singapore. And I've lost him.''

The explanation seemed enough for Emily Morrison. She picked up her baby and May followed her into the woods with the bucket of water.

The walk was longer than May expected. After a while they turned down toward the river again and at last came to a snug, newly-built log shanty, close to the water. It was partially hidden behind dense shrubs and trees. A canoe was docked in a small cove in front of it. Behind the house were rows of tall stakes pounded into the ground to create a shelter for the animals and the garden.

''Bring the water inside,'' Emily called as she pulled open a heavy oaken plank door that swung on big iron hinges. The living-room inside was plain but cosy and clean.

Baby Jonathan had fallen asleep and his mother settled him snugly into a cradle by the fireplace, where a large black kettle hung above some glowing logs. Emily opened the lid and poured a cup of water into it from the bucket.

''We brought the rocking chair, the cradle and the wooden chest from Boston,'' said Emily with open pride as she swept her hand over the room.

''And you have three glass windows,'' said May, imagining that glass must be a precious pioneer luxury.

''Aren't they beautiful?'' Emily wiped one of them with a cloth. ''They cost us a pretty penny at the store in Singapore.''

Through the remainder of the day, the two girls

worked together, May rocking and tending the lively baby while Emily milked the cow and managed to catch several fish for their evening meal. May gave shrewd advice for the garden and helped plant corn and pumpkin seeds.

Along the shanty walls May was surprised to find a barrel of flour, a barrel of salt, a half barrel of pickled pork, a keg of honey and a stock of dried meat. Emily's husband was indeed a good provider even though he left her on her own.

Once as they planted seeds in the garden with a clumsy stick for digging holes, May said thoughtlessly, "You should have this land ploughed with a power machine."

Emily looked up sharply. "I don't know what you're talking about. It doesn't seem like you belong here, May. And those funny clothes you wear — my husband, Thomas, wouldn't like them. He's fussy about the way a woman should look. Do many girls in Canada dress like that?"

"A few," May answered limply, promising herself that she would have to leave before Thomas returned.

However, by evening the two of them were laughing together as old friends, and were settled comfortably at a rude board table to eat bowls of stew from the kettle. Suddenly May cried out in alarm. In each of the windows were dusky-faced Indians staring at them. May expected Emily to reach for one of the rifles that hung on the wall.

"You shouldn't be afraid, May." For the first time there was aloofness in Emily's voice. "They are Indians too."

May didn't answer. How could she tell Emily that this experience was as new and frightening to her as it must have been for Emily when she first saw them? She began to wonder how she was going to live among these dark-skinned, staring faces.

"I'm sorry, May," Emily said quickly. "You look like an Indian girl, that's all. I was afraid too when I first saw all these faces. They come night after night. Now I'm accustomed to them and I know they are just friendly and curious."

"That's all?" May couldn't believe it.

"Oh, the Indians are my nearest neighbours and friends, May." Emily began gathering up the dishes and stoking the fire so that it wouldn't go out during the night. She led May to a small room off the living-room. The floor was covered with bear skins.

"We'll sleep here, May, and I'll pull the cradle in beside us." Emily laughed happily. "It's so good to have company. But, May, don't be surprised when you wake up in the morning and find two or three Indians rolled up in their blankets and lying in front of the fire. They won't harm us — they just want to share the warmth of the fireplace. I never lock the door."

Emily yawned and was soon asleep.

May stared and stared into the dark room.

8

The next morning, as Emily had predicted, an Indian man and woman rose silently and expressionless from the floor before the fireplace like genies rising mysteriously upward. They were wrapped in bright-coloured blankets and the man wore a fur turban on his head.

They had started to leave when Emily said quickly,

"Is the friend you lost an Indian, May? These two might know him. What is his name?"

"Lee Pokagon," May called from the bearskin-covered room.

"Chief Pokagon!" The Indians were astonished and said the name in unison.

"Where — is — he?" Emily asked the question slowly.

"He is great man." The Indian man stumbled over the words. "Known in Singapore. Ask there." The two turned with sweeping dignity and left the room.

"I guess you'll find him in Singapore, May. Is he really a chief?" Emily yawned sleepily, picking up screaming Jonathan who wanted to be fed. "Now that you know where to find him, you'll probably leave soon. I wish you could stay."

May's mind was in wild turmoil. The ghostly chief was named Pokagon — no doubt an ancient relative of Lee's. He was known in Singapore, so she should leave for Singapore at once.

A crash of splitting wood sounded outdoors and when

May and Emily looked out the window they saw that the cow was loose. She had broken down one of the stakes and was ambling toward the river.

"Oh May," Emily cried. "Take care of Jonathan. I'll have to get a rope and tie Bessie to a tree and repair the fence right away."

How could she leave Emily now? Feeling that the burden of her responsibilities had to be shared, May decided to stay another day.

One crisis followed another until early afternoon when another strange sound caught the ears of the two girls. This time it was the neighing of a horse and the shrill whistle of a cardinal.

Emily ran to the door of the shanty, her eyes bright and her face as radiant as the spring sun.

"It's Thomas," she shouted. She picked up Jonathan and ran outside.

Thomas, who was fussy about women's clothes, had returned. It was time for May to leave — and quickly. She scribbled a note on an open tablet on the table.

> You will always be my friend, Emily.
> Thank you for the board and room.
> May

Then she left the cosy pine-log home by the back door, headed for the river and turned in the direction of Singapore. It had been a happy visit in the pioneer shanty and she would treasure it always.

After walking a short distance May wasn't surprised to hear the rolling wheels of a farm wagon and the clomping hooves of horses above her. There must be a road at the top of the dune. There would have to be one to unload the waiting logs. The wagon stopped and May saw a large, husky, black-bearded man come crashing through the woods toward her. She thought of hiding, but it was too late.

"Hey there, boy!" The man's voice was as resounding as a trumpet.

What does he mean by "boy"? May thought. Then she remembered that pants were not worn by girls here. Also her black hair was bobbed and hung loose about her face.

By now the bearded man was face to face with her. His red plaid flannel shirt was patched and faded and his hands were black with dirt. His heavy pants were tucked into spiked boots. May could not see into his eyes for thick black eyebrows settled on his lower forehead like giant cockroaches. What did such a man want with her?

"Speak English?" he asked.

He thinks I'm an Indian. May was annoyed as well as frightened.

"Of course I speak English," she answered standing straight and tall in spite of her growing terror.

The man was puzzled. "You're a strange one all right. I ain't never seen the likes of you around these parts. Your face is Indian, but your clothes aren't. But you'll do."

He clamped his big hand around May's arm and began dragging her up the hill toward his wagon.

May was terrified. She tried pulling back and releasing herself, but it was no use. The burly man's fingers were bands of steel around her arm.

They climbed onto the wagon seat together. May twisted and turned and finally cried out:

"What right have you to pull me into this wagon? Where are you taking me?"

The man kept his grip on her, holding the reins with

the other hand and flicking them to get the horses started.

"I'm takin' you to Smith's Lumber Camp back in the woods." The man's voice boomed out loudly and sounded as if it was coming out of his nose. "It's spring and thawin' time and the loggin's almost done. Some of the shanty boys skipped off for merrymakin' in Singapore until the River Drive." He stopped talking briefly to wipe his nose with the back of his hand.

"The cook's helper went along and didn't come back. So the boss is mad and says to me, 'Git me a boy today to fill his boots.' And that boy is you."

"But I don't want to be a cook's helper," May protested. Her arm was beginning to hurt.

"You ain't got no say, boy, when Big Bill McGrew picks you up off the road." The man grinned and loosened his grip. "The man-catcher they call me." He smirked. "You've just been kidnapped, laddie."

"Kidnapped!" May was stunned. She could not react at first. She didn't want to talk or listen further; she just knew she would have to escape somehow as quickly as possible. She tried moving slowly to the edge of the seat where she could jump from the wagon, but Big Bill grabbed her arm and yanked her back close to him.

They jogged along in silence. McGrew produced a pipe and puffed clouds of smoke in all directions, destroying the bracing fragrance of fresh pine.

The dark, majestic forest closed in on them, the massive straight trunks rising like sculptured monuments. For a moment May remembered Uncle Steve telling her how white pine wood was clean and strong and easy to handle. It was straight-grained and wouldn't splinter when nails went through. No wonder all the mills were greedy for its lumber.

A shaft of light cut across the bumpy road as if a curtain had been pulled back from a stage. In front of May, as far as she could see, were ugly hills of tree stumps and in between them the land was burned. It was a cemetery of dead trees!

How could these loggers cut every tree and then burn the ground? May was appalled. The Appleby Nursery guarded and protected trees. They were sacred to Aunt Nell and Uncle Steve. Trees produced oxygen and helped make clean air; they gave shade and beauty to the countryside.

"Don't you know anything about conservation?" May shouted. All traces of her shyness disappeared in her present anger. She decided that the burly man beside her was not only a crook but stupid. "How could the men in this camp cut down every tree and then burn the ground?"

McGrew's cockroach eyebrows pulled together.

"Shut yuh mouth," he ordered with the pipe still between his teeth. "I never heard such crazy talk. . . . We burn up the slashings in this camp. Smith don't want no chips and limbs and brush left behind on his land." He gave May an added yank on her sore arm. "Cuttin' the trees lets a little daylight into these swamps."

"That's really stupid," May said. "How can the trees grow again in burned-over land? And don't you know unprotected top soil washes away? This sandy dune-land will crumble right into Lake Michigan someday because it isn't held down."

McGrew gave May a disgusted shove away from him. "They must have sprung you loose from a nut house. . . . If you don't shut up like I said, I'll turn you over my knee and whack the living daylights out of yuh."

Then May remembered. It must be about the spring of

1835 or 1840 because Uncle Steve had told her most of the white pine was gone from Michigan by 1850 — skimmed right off like cream from a milk can. May shuddered. But there was no use talking to this man. Why couldn't they cut every other tree? This must be the way a bombed city looks with just the foundations sticking up. There aren't any birds or people after bombs hit, May thought sadly, just like here.

9

Far in the distance, May saw smoke rising like a single thread in the vast open sky and knew they must be coming to the lumber camp. Behind the smoke was a backdrop of uncut towering pines. She was determined to keep her lips sealed and make no more attempts to slide from the wagon seat. How could she ever escape unseen over these endless acres of tree stumps? Perhaps later when some of the loggers went to Singapore she could hide in their wagon and ride along.

It was as though McGrew had read her mind. He pointed ahead toward two long, rough buildings with smaller lean-to's nearby. They were built of yellow peeled logs with the spaces in between stuffed with mud and clay. The smell of pine was everywhere. Two black iron kettles swung over an open fire of crackling logs.

"That's the Cook's Shanty," McGrew shouted pointing to the building near the fire. "The other one's the bunk house for the shantyboys." He headed toward the open fire.

"I've hired yuh now, boy, and yuh'll git your pay when the River Log Drives are done. Try to run away an' I'll chain yuh to a stake."

McGrew jerked the horses to a stop and jumped from the wagon pulling May behind him. "Yuh do just what Cook O'Toole says. We call him 'Taters. Now git." He shoved her through the main door.

Before them was a long pine-log room. Two narrow tables ran down the length of it covered with yellow oil-cloth and lined on either side were split log benches without backs. A cast-iron stove in the middle radiated heat from burning pine logs. Kerosene lamps hung from the ceiling.

At the far end of the room was the kitchen. Kettles on big black stoves steamed and bubbled. Rising biscuit dough covered an enormous white sanded work-table.

The room was designed for one purpose — eating.

A giant tub of a man entered from the kitchen door. He was wrapped in a white apron that split at the seams and a white cook's hat that tilted on top of a tangled mass of curly black hair. One massive hair-covered arm reached out to open and close a steaming oven door. The other hand held a meat chopper the size of a tree axe.

Big Bill McGrew, who no longer looked so big, marched up and slammed him on the back.

"I snatched yuh a cook's helper, Taters," he cried out.

Taters swung around like a circus elephant with one foot on a stool. Rolls of fat rippled from his cheeks over his neck and chest and down into his stomach. But the most startling feature was his deep blue eyes that sparkled with laughter. Looking into them May lost all fear of the man.

He sized May up, pointing the meat chopper in her direction. Then, as Bill McGrew slipped out the kitchen door, there was a rumble of laughter.

"You're the cook's helper — ho ho. I never in me life saw such a skinny slip of a lad. . . . A twig of a tree y'are in a lumber camp, and what can ye possibly do to help feed sixty boys who eat like steers that are starvin'."

May liked the lilt of his talk and the way all his sentences ended like questions, but she was angry that he should make such fun of her.

"I think I should tell you, Mr. O'Toole," May said looking him directly in the eyes, "I'm not a lad. I'm a girl and my name is May and I didn't want to come here at all. I was kidnapped!"

The laughter stopped and the fat rippling cheeks that were bright red from the oven blanched white and sagged.

"A girl?" This time Taters' sentence really was a question.

May nodded.

"I believe y'are tellin' me the truth," the cook said, turning back to his work-table. "There's no time for talkin' now." He began chopping great slabs of red meat. "I'll tell ye this though, May; I'll take care of ye and treat ye like me own daughter, but ye'll have to work hard and ye can't leave until the River Log Run is over."

"How long is that?" May asked thinking she would probably have to accept this offer.

Taters picked her up and sat her on a high stool behind the kitchen partition. He pulled over a barrel of potatoes and placed a peeling knife beside her.

"Two or three weeks at least," he answered, motioning that she should start peeling the potatoes.

"Three weeks!" May was shocked. "I can't stay that long." She thought of Lee and the Indian chief and her urgent need to find both of them.

O'Toole merely shrugged his massive shoulders. "Big Bill catches anyone who tries to run away. He's mean — mean as a grizzly bear." He turned around and gave

May a long, hard look. "We won't share this news about ye bein' a girl with him or anyone else."

May resentfully agreed.

There was silence between them as May peeled until her fingers were stiff and her skin had taken on the brownish look of the growing mound of potato peelings. One high window was the only means of ventilation and light. Out of it May could see the pointed tops of the pines that would soon be sent crashing to the ground by the logger's axe. The sky above them was growing dark.

Rivulets of perspiration ran down O'Toole's face. His work had reached a fever pitch, for the shantyboys would soon be coming in. They had been felling trees from dawn until dusk.

"There's nothin' wrong with the shantyboys." O'Toole sounded uneasy as he called to May from the outside kettles where he was dishing up chunks of meat, turnips and peas into washpan-size serving dishes. "The boys just don't use too nice language." O'Toole paused. "But they're a hard workin' bunch — there's some Irishmen like me, some Swedes and Finns, Yankees from the woods of Maine, and Michigan farmers who need work for the winter."

O'Toole began to laugh. "The veteran loggers come from Canada — Nova Scotia, New Brunswick, Prince Edward Island, Upper Canada." He burst forth with his low 'ho ho'. "The ones with the high spirits are the 'Canucks' from Quebec. Ye can't miss them with their red sashes and their French talk."

May was stationed at the stove frying mountains of sliced potatoes — "taters", as O'Toole called them. Rows of apple pies appeared on the work-table with plates of freshly baked biscuits.

"These boys work their fingers to the bone," O'Toole explained, proudly displaying the abundance of food, "and eatin' is their pleasure. They'll always sign up to work in a camp with a cook the likes of me." His blue eyes twinkled.

Suddenly from the open kitchen door came a bursting noise of screeching wagon wheels, neighing horses, the shouts and cries and laughter of men. The doors of the Kitchen Shanty swung open and the heavy-booted shantyboys poured in, sliding onto the benches, elbowing room for themselves, bending over the tables, piling food from the passing serving bowls into mountains on their plates and then shovelling it, with gargantuan spoonfuls, into their mouths. There was little conversation as they ate.

May watched with unbelieving eyes until Taters caught her by the shoulder and stationed her behind the kitchen wall to cut the pies.

At last, with their stomachs overloaded, the men slid from their eating benches and headed for the long Bunk House nearby.

May slumped over the work-table, almost too tired to eat her own dinner which O'Toole pushed in front of her.

"Ye'll have to scour the table top and kettle bottoms with sand before ye gets a wink of sleep," Taters said, rotating his heavy body around the kitchen again like an agile circus elephant. "I'll fix ye a private room right here by the stove," he said, "and ye'll have a corn husk mattress and a blanket just like the men."

May could have slept on the floor without either of them.

The food, however, was delicious. May hoped all the

vitamins and minerals would flow from it into her body and give her the strength of a logger. Surely there would be no more jobs after the scouring?

As she worked, the sound of singing came through the high open window in the Cook's Shanty.

A strong, resonant tenor sang:

A is for Ax, and that we all know,
And B is for Boy that can use it also;
C is for Chopping we first do begin,
And D is for Danger we often fall in.

Then a chorus joined him singing:

So merry, so merry are we,
No mortals on earth are as happy as we.
T' me I derry O derry I derry down,
Use shantyboys well and there's nothing
goes wrong.

May began humming with them as they sang the verses over and over getting louder with each chorus.

"That's Willy from New Brunswick doin' the solos," Taters commented proudly. "There's a split log 'deacon's bench' runs down the length of the bunk house. The boys sit on it of an evening and sing, dance a few jigs, fight a little, play cards, and dry their wet socks on a criss-cross o' lines above them." He laughed. "They fall into their bunks for a night's sleep with all their clothes on."

"But, Mr. O'Toole," May interrupted, feeling she could speak some of her thoughts to this good-natured man. "If your boys cut down every tree as they are doing now and leave the fields full of stumps, they won't have jobs very long."

May realized the answer before Mr. O'Toole could open his mouth. She'd read about it once in a history book. Many of the early pioneers saw the unploughed fields and uncut forests of the New World as a wilderness that stretched on and on forever. When the forests of Michigan were destroyed, they would pick up the saws from their mills, take their axes and their songs, move a notch west, and cut some more forests.

"They suck out the gold from this land and then move on to find some more," Taters said, sounding almost merry.

May couldn't believe this jovial man could give his blessing to such selfish destruction.

"That isn't fair, Mr. O'Toole," she exploded. "What about trees for the next generation and then the next — and besides your loggers are stealing the Indians' hunting grounds."

"Such talk, girl." Taters appeared dumbfounded. "Wealth is for those who know how to get it. Trees are for those who know how to log them. . . . As for the Indians — a few o' them work on the River Log Drive. But for the lot o' them, May, they hardly use the land at all. Didn't ye know the government is movin' all the Michigan Indians west of the great Mississippi?"

He looked at May strangely.

"Ye wouldn't have Indian blood in your veins, would ye, May?"

May didn't answer. She was shocked and dismayed by his unfeeling talk, but she was also worried. If the government was moving all the Indians west, Lee would go with them and she would never find him. She would have to try to run away tomorrow night even at the risk of being caught by Bill McGrew. She would make plans all day tomorrow while she worked.

The solo singer from the bunk house began a slow,

plaintive song. He almost sobbed the words that came through the open kitchen door:

There's many a young Canadian boy leaves home
  and friends so dear,
And longing for experiment to Michigan to steer.
In less than three months after, a telegram does
  come,
Saying, "Your son was killed in the lumbering
  woods, his body we'll send home."

The verses went on and on with Taters humming the tune and from time to time wiping tears from his eyes. At the end, the corpse of the boy, whose name was Harry Dunne, was shipped home, bringing "death from grieving to both his dad and mum and a curse on the woods of Michigan."

"A curse on the woods of Michigan." May found herself humming the refrain as she fell exhausted onto the cornhusk mattress, still wearing all her clothes.

10

May woke the next morning to the clanging of Cook O'Toole's iron triangle as he stood outside the kitchen door, hitting the instrument with all the strength of his mammoth arm. May opened her eyes in alarm. It was still dark. Was she back at the Flower Shop in Sarnia? Was this her nightmare in which all the twisted pipes, long smoke stacks and oil drums of Chemical Valley exploded? Were ringing fire engines coming to the rescue? She jumped from her hard, bumpy mattress and ran to the door.

"Good mornin' to ye, May," said Taters, his red, rippling face illuminated by light from the ever-burning log fire below the black iron kettles.

"What's happening?" she asked, running her fingers through her straight black hair to smooth out the tangles.

"Why it's four o'clock, me lassie, time for all good shantyboys to be up for breakfast and off to work."

"Four o'clock!" May was incredulous. But the men were shuffling into the Cook's Shanty, eating the breakfast Taters had laid out for them and washing it down with burning hot coffee. A few of them lingered at the long oilcloth-covered tables.

May joined Taters at the outdoor fire, grateful for its warmth since the air was cold enough to make smoke of her breath. She noticed that the men coming out of the kitchen wore jackets, knitted caps and double-knitted mittens with long wrists. Most of them had patches of deerskin on the palms of their mittens.

"Deerskin is best for grippin' an axe," Taters told her. The men gave May scant notice, making remarks like, "Got yourself a skinny Indian boy for a helper, Taters?"

"Scrapin' the bottom of the barrel to find a cookee, eh?" a red-sashed Quebecker asked, tweaking May's cheek. Taters slapped his hand.

A giant of a man followed him, also wearing the red sash of a Quebecker. He matched Cook O'Toole's girth, but his body was made up of muscle instead of fat. There wasn't a spark of laughter in his eyes, just beady stubbornness. A red knitted cap stretched over his bull-like head. He looked like he had been hewn directly from the trunk of a virgin pine tree and May automatically shrank back from him.

The man who had just pinched May turned around and laughed at the giant.

"Tryin' to scare the wisp of a cook's helper, are yuh, Joe?"

The giant Joe growled, lowered his head and butted the man across the camp yard.

No one uttered a sound, but after he thundered away Taters turned to May and whispered, "See what I told ye, lassie. Some of the shantyboys are a tough lot. That's why it's best, since you're a girl, to stay away from them. I've seen Joe Fournier butt down a heavy door with his head when it wouldn't open."

Gradually the men piled themselves into horse-drawn sleighs and headed for the woods that rimmed the barren stump-covered yard. May decided she couldn't walk as far as the forest tonight. When she left the camp, she would have to follow what the men called the "Tote Road" that led to the river across the burned-over land. There would be no hiding places unless the moon took cover behind a cloud.

She noticed Big Bill McGrew prancing around the edges of the camp on horseback like a police guard. The sight of him made May edgy. Was he on patrol day *and* night?

She had already stored away some biscuits under her mattress and decided to take the one blanket Taters had given her. It would be payment for two days' work, she thought, easing her conscience on the matter of stealing.

Taters swung into action, perching May again on the stool behind the kitchen partition with another barrel of potatoes. May groaned, but was thankful to have a job that kept her off her feet. She needed to rest them for tonight's long walk.

As May began peeling she heard voices on the opposite side of the partition. Two men were talking leisurely and they weren't shantyboys. Their speech was more polished, like the speech of her teachers at Sarnia Secondary School. She wondered whether they could be the owners of the lumber camp.

"Did you get the branding hammer to stamp an 'S' on the end of all the logs?" a man with a deep voice asked.

"Right here in my bag," a high-voiced man answered.

S for Smith's Lumber Camp, of course, May said to herself. She listened intently. She could hear them sipping coffee.

"We'll float all our logs down to the Singapore Mill. It's a boom town all right. . . . The folks there say it's going to equal Detroit and Chicago one of these days."

Then the high-voiced man changed the subject. "Did

you see that six-foot, handsome-looking Indian chief walking through the town yesterday? The people say he's educated and well liked.''

''That would be Leopold Pokagon of the Potawatomi.''

May jumped, cutting her finger on the peeling knife. She wrapped it quickly with a rag: she didn't want Taters to see the blood and interrupt this conversation.

Chief Leopold Pokagon! Imagine! May was excited. Lee's name was almost the same. No wonder they looked alike. The chief was probably a long, long-ago great-grandfather.

May quietly edged her stool closer to the partition, peeling as fast as she could, so Taters wouldn't shift her to another job.

These men were really interested in the chief. May's heart thumped furiously. The deep-voiced one was telling the other that Pokagon was the son of a Chippewa father and an Ottawa mother. In his youth he had been a fierce fighter.

A fierce fighter? May questioned this in her mind, remembering the sad white-haired man on the streets of Saugatuck.

The deep-voiced man went on with his information. Once in battle, he said, Pokagon had been captured by Topenebee of the Potawatomi who liked him and called him Pokagon, the Indian name for rib. This was because he wore the rib of a chief he had slain as part of his headgear. He married into the Potawatomi tribe and became their next chief.

''A warrior — a real rib,'' May repeated under her breath.

''The chief was asking a strange question on the streets of Singapore yesterday,'' said the high-voiced man abruptly. "He speaks English and he was looking for a lost Indian girl. May Appleby is her name apparently. She wears her hair like a boy and dresses in pants."

May leaned so far forward that she tipped her stool and fell headfirst into the potato barrel. The cloth bandage from her cut finger flew off and drops of blood dripped onto the floor.

The two men peered round the door, then left.

"A clumsy cook's helper," she heard them comment on their way out.

Taters soared into the kitchen, pulling May from the barrel, setting her upright on the stool and bandaging her cut finger properly.

"What a fix ye've got yourself into, May, me girl." He shook his head in despair. "Go outside now and stir the food in the kettles — and if ye fall into one of those, the boys will eat ye for supper."

May was glad of the fresh air and for a chance to think over what she had just heard. Chief Pokagon's need to find her must be urgent. May wondered if she should give herself up to Mr. Smith, the owner. But this would arouse suspicion about why she was in the camp and the shantyboys would then know she was a girl. She weighed the possibilities. It seemed best, after all, to follow her first plan and run away as soon as it was dark.

May hardly spoke during the long afternoon, following every command that Taters made. He talked endlessly about his fellow loggers, calling the men who chopped through giant trees with a single-bitten axe Fallers and telling May how they cut away the branches and hitched the main log to a horse which slid it over icy ground to a loading site and then later lifted it with other logs onto a large bobsled that hauled them to the river.

"Listen, May." Taters pointed behind them towards the forest. A far-away cry echoed through the air like an eerie warning: "Tim — m — ber." In the forest the pointed top of the tallest pine began to sway. Then its huge straight trunk arched downward. There was a distant sound like thunder as the giant tree crashed to the ground.

May felt an aching pain inside her stomach for she knew that every majestic tree in the surrounding forest — not only the pines but the walnuts, the sugar maples, the sassafras, the birches, the oak — was destined to be chopped and logged and carted away. Why didn't these loggers think? Why didn't they select some trees to cut and leave others to grow to even greater heights.

Even jolly, hard-working Taters, who cared for her as best he knew how, was caught up in this feverish tree cutting.

"That might be the last tree logged for the season," he said sadly. Then he brightened. "Now the River Log Rolling will begin!"

Standing on a bench, May stirred the great kettles that were cooking gravy. Tonight the feast would be thick rare steaks, potatoes and plenty of gravy. Taters was emptying his larder in preparation for the closing of the Winter Logging Camp.

As May poured her peeled potatoes into the large iron kettle out of doors where they would cook later for evening supper, the sun shone bright and warm and a gentle breeze began to blow as though heralding an early summer. May breathed deeply, expecting the rich scent of violets, trillium and lilac buds. Instead, she breathed in the clean, bracing smell of pine.

Taters pushed himself through the kitchen door, sniffing the air and shaking his head.

''Too warm for this time o' year.'' He squashed his foot over a spot of melting ice. ''The boys will be loadin' the bobsled with the last logs of the season and haulin' them to the river before the sun goes down.''

''When will they eat, Mr. O'Toole?'' May was worried. She was hoping for an early meal and a speedy getaway.

''Late, girl, very, very late,'' Taters continued to shake his head. He wet the end of his finger and held it up to the breeze.

''A warm wind'll be blowin' through the night too.'' He hummed a jolly tune and began to roll his body with the rhythm. ''We'll be assemblin' our kitchen tonight May and movin' it to the river.''

''To the river!'' May's mouth dropped open.

She listened with dismay as Taters outlined the work ahead of them. When the Rolling Drive began on the melted, even-flowing Kalamazoo River and the piles of logs along its banks tumbled one after another into its waters, the cook and his helper would board a makeshift kitchen — a ''wanigan'', Taters called it — built on a raft, that would float along behind the logs.

At night, it seemed, sleeping tents and the floating Cook's Shanty would pull up alongside the river bank and another famous O'Toole outsize meal would be served.

''Along the river we'll be servin' a different crew, May.'' Taters was already stashing pots and pans into the back of a horse-drawn wagon. ''It's River Hogs and the Jam Crew that'll be fillin' their empty stomachs. The Loggers will bid us goodbye and head for a night in Singapore. I'll not be seein' them again till another season.''

''Then what happens to you and to me?'' May was wide-eyed.

"Why, May, ye don't seem to know a thing." Taters looked at her strangely again but the look was mingled with affection.

"We'll follow the boys while they guide the logs down the river and keep them from jammin' up, until they deliver them to the Boom Company. . . . Then Smith Lumber Company gives us our pay. You go your way and I go mine."

The strange names were like a different language to May — River Hogs, Jam Crews, Boom Companies. But there was no way she could escape this new turn of events. The warmer weather had destroyed all possibility of running away tonight. The Tote Road to the Kalamazoo River would be filled with wagons, sleighs, neighing horses, a travelling kitchen, shantyboys, the cook and his "slip of a helper".

At least we will be moving in the right direction, May thought — toward Singapore.

11

By early evening a sleigh appeared near the camp on the Tote Road, loaded so high with logs that May thought the man sitting on top of them, holding the reins of two straining horses, would surely fall to the ground.

"Don't even breath when he goes by, May," Taters warned. "Many a Loader has met his death with one false move and found himself crushed under tumbling logs."

The Loader didn't blink an eyelash as he drove by. He was heading straight for the river and the high log rollways. Taters explained that to make the pull easier for the horses, men called Icers had covered the road ahead with water that would freeze. To keep the hard-working animals from slipping too much, the horses had been shod with heavy caulked shoes.

What if the water doesn't freeze? May wondered. But there was no time to worry about the man. It was dinner time for the Loggers. They were rough and boisterous, eager to be packed and moving. The food disappeared with such speed May was certain they hadn't chewed a bite of it. They laughed and yelled and slapped one another with noisy goodbyes.

Even the giant hammer-head, Joe Fournier, had a slight smile on his face. At last they were off — "scattered over the face of the earth", Taters said — until another winter and another logging camp. The sudden quiet when the last one left was eerie.

The moon rose, full and orange, with no cloud to blot out its light. It was as though it had been turned on like a light bulb to help with the work and to prevent all sleep. The job took all night. It was not until the pink light of sunrise that Taters' kitchen wagon pulled slowly away from the camp.

Several times black-bearded Bill McGrew had marched by, checking to see if May was earning her pay. May scoured each kettle and sanded the work table to a silky smoothness before she climbed wearily into the wagon seat beside Taters. Before he shouted ''Gid-diup'' to the team of horses, her head fell against his huge soft shoulder and she slept. . . .

Sounds of screams, shouts, crashing wood and splashing water jarred May awake. She found herself alone in the kitchen wagon high above the Kalamazoo. Beneath her, logs that had been piled all winter against posts in the ground along the steep rise of ground above the river had been unleashed and were rolling one after another down the rollways into the churning river where men with long spiked peavies jumped from log to log like grasshoppers pushing and tugging to untangle the jammed-up logs.

May looked about for Taters and finally spotted him trying to balance himself on the wanigan, the wide raft that was being outfitted with cooking stoves and a work table.

May wondered what she should do in the confusion of all the noise and activity. It occurred to her that she could easily run away. Everyone was so busy they wouldn't notice her. She could follow the river to Singapore.

Then she thought of McGrew, who might catch up with her and give her the beating he had threatened, and of Taters, who would be left without a helper. Even with his short-sighted outlook on life, he had been kind to her. She shuddered to imagine what might have happened if she had been left in the hands of her kidnapper.

May concluded that she should stay with Taters until they got to Singapore.

She saw him roll a barrel of potatoes onto the raft. He looked up and motioned her to join him. More potatoes, she sighed, as she started to clamber down. Her fingers were already calloused where she held the knife.

The day was not fair and balmy as everyone had expected, but was now dark with a rising wind. The clouds were gray and skittish in the sky.

''It could storm, May.'' Taters frowned as he greeted her. ''Then we'll be rockin' back and forth on the water behind the rollin' logs. There's nothing we can do to stop them now.''

More logs were pouring into the river, making a waterfall of pounding wood, like an avalanche shaking the earth's foundation.

Suddenly a startled cry came from above.

''A River Hog in the water!''

Looking down river May saw a man's head bobbing between two logs. He'll be crushed. May clutched the tottering stove on the raft. But another man, riding the logs, speared one of them with his peavy pole, shoved it to the side and yanked the fallen man upward. Dripping wet, the River Hog swayed for an instant and then gained his footing. Soon he was jumping from log to log again, guiding them down the river.

''He's a mighty lucky man.'' Taters laughed his hearty ''ho, ho'' and, weaving back and forth himself, stepped onto the middle of the kitchen raft.

May wasn't so amused. She didn't even like the name given to the spiked-shoed River Hogs.

''What if we get caught between some logs

ourselves?" she asked, almost wishing now that she *had* run away.

"Oh, don't worry your head about that, May." Taters was still shaking with laughter. "We won't set sail on our wanigan until every log from the rollway is toppled and splashing in the water."

May was relieved, but not for long. One of the falling logs jammed against a rock in the water and stuck. Masses of logs began piling behind it in a groaning, dangerous mound. May hung onto the camp stove again.

Instantly a young "Whitewater Boy", as Taters called him, clambered onto the wild tangle. He seemed to know exactly what he was doing and was as sure-footed as a squirrel jumping from limb to limb in the waving branches of a tree.

"He'll have to get that key log dynamited, May, or you and I and the wanigan will be buried." The laughter had left Taters' face and it was almost as white as the foam on the turbulent water.

May watched the young man with horrified wonder. He bent quickly and planted a lighted dynamite stick beside the blocked log. Then he jumped onto the top of the piling logs, balancing himself precariously. One foot slipped and he began to scramble.

"He's a goner," Taters groaned. "They'll bury him on the river bank, cut his name in the bark of a tree and hang his boot on a limb overhead."

"No, he's not, Mr. O'Toole!" May shouted. "Look — he made it to the shore."

May's words were lost in a roaring explosion. Bits and pieces of wood flew skyward.

"The logs are breaking!" a nearby River Hog called to

his comrades, as the river was transformed into a foaming, thundering sluice of water and logs.

It was some time before Taters and May regained their composure and set their kitchen in order again. May found her potato peeler. Now and then, to steady herself and to rest her eyes and ears from the pounding logs, May glanced at the opposite bank where the steep dunes were still covered by quiet green forest. Not far down the river, May realized, was Mount Baldhead which she and Lee had passed only a few days ago. She wondered if there would still be Potawatomi there from the spring celebration. If she saw one of them now she wouldn't hesitate to greet him.

As May looked, a tall single feather darted up and down among the pine needles. It couldn't be a bird: it was too large and too upright. She dropped her peeling knife and stared. The feather was fastened to the headgear of an Indian. She could see his blurred face. And just below him, anchored near the shore, were several birch bark canoes.

Just as May lifted her hand to wave, a crack of thunder shook the sky.

"Come along, May," Taters cried, motioning her to settle on the raft. "The log rolling is almost finished. We've got to pull up the anchor and follow."

May grabbed the heavy potato barrel. Rain splashed down suddenly and she dived under the makeshift wooden shelter over the cooking stove. It was too small for O'Toole. The rain and wind blew off his cook's hat and flattened the mass of black curls that covered his pumpkin-shaped head. The water around them roared with increasing speed and the strong wind started to blow up large waves.

May grabbed an oar that Taters handed her and paddled with all her strength to keep the raft from crashing into the bank. Taters did the same. Then an unexpected, forgotten log broke loose from the high dune. It was heading straight for the raft.

"Jump," Taters called. May saw him fall with a great splash into the river. She dived in after him. Within seconds the raft had splintered, and pieces of wood, pans, pots and potatoes circled in the water around them.

On the opposite shore May saw the Indian with the blurred face and tall feather jump into his canoe and head like a arrow in her direction.

"May the Lord help me," Taters spluttered, "I can't swim."

May swam toward him but his flailing arms pushed her away. The Indian was beside her now. He reached out quickly and without a word grabbed her arm and pulled her into his canoe.

"May," he cried hoarsely, "I've searched every place for you. Are you all right?"

May looked at him, amazed. It was Lee. She was overwhelmed with relief and joy. If they hadn't been rocking about wildly in a log-jammed river she would have grabbed him and hugged him. His appearance, however, shocked her for he was wearing soft deerskin Indian clothes, with moccasins on his feet and in his headband the tall feather.

"Help!" A desperate wail came from Taters as his head disappeared under the water.

"Help him, Lee." May was frightened. "He's my friend."

"Take my paddle, May. Edge up close to him. I'll grab his head and hold it above water, then we'll aim for the shore. . . . He's too heavy to pull aboard."

Lee was confident and sure of himself. May noticed fleetingly that the cynical bitterness that had been part of his expression seemed to have disappeared.

As they drew near Taters' bobbing head, Lee leaned from the canoe, grabbed him under the chin and held his head above water as May paddled hard toward the shore.

Miraculously, the canoe, Taters' great hulking body, Lee and May all landed safely on a narrow stretch of sand.

Taters spluttered and coughed and shook his hands and feet like a shaggy oversized dog.

"Blessed be the saints, May," he managed to say, his massive chest heaving for added breath. "An Indian lad has saved us. And here I've been sayin' they were a wild bunch of heathens."

12

On the opposite bank of the river, a lone horseback rider dashed back and forth in nervous alarm. He had watched the smashing of the kitchen raft and had spotted O'Toole on the sandbar with May and Lee.

"I'm swimmin' over for you, O'Toole," he called, cupping one hand around his mouth. "Grab that boy. Don't let him escape with the Indian!"

May recognized that blaring voice at once. Bill McGrew was fording the river on his horse. He intended to see that she stayed with Taters, and would use his gun if necessary to chase Lee away.

Taters guessed what she was thinking. He was breathing normally now and was standing up.

"May," he said looking at her intently and also keeping an eye on the advancing McGrew. "There's somethin' strange about ye and this Indian lad here. It's like ye came from another place."

He hesitated and then became nervous for McGrew and his horse were midway across the river. Also it was continuing to rain and they were already soaked. Taters stood over May trying to shelter her.

"I had a daughter once who died in Ireland." He paused. "I thought, May, that ye might take her place. But the two of ye saved my life and I am grateful. Now take this sharp peeling knife, May, as something to remember me by, and be off with this fine-looking Indian lad."

Lee stood away from the two of them and was silent.

May reached for the knife and put it in the pocket of her jeans. As she did so she felt several stones and pebbles that she had picked up from the polluted water off Singing Sands Beach. One of the stones was smooth and polished. May held it out to Taters.

"It's a Petoskey Stone, Mr. O'Toole," she said. "It's fossilized coral from the place I come from, and some people say it was formed 350 million years ago. You could probably find some around here, but this one is polished."

Taters was pleased.

"Why, thank you," he said. "Now be off with ye fast." And he shoved them toward the canoe.

Lee jumped into the bow and grabbed his oar.

"Lie down flat in the bottom, May," he said in an urgent voice. "The man on the horse has a gun."

May obeyed. The water swished under her in a rhythmic beat with Lee's rowing. Tall, thin grassy blades of wild rice swept gently over her back. Muffled cries came from the sandbar and she heard Taters shout, "Oh, let the lad go. He was no help at all to me."

"Bless him," May said aloud into the strong bent cedar boughs at the bottom of the boat. Taters pays little attention to the world around him, she thought: his eyes are buried in his cast-iron cooking kettle; but he does have a big, generous heart and he was good to me.

May remembered the old man on the river near present-day Saugatuck with his snake-like cane. He was going to hide the sickness of Singing Sands Beach behind a row of trees; if he didn't see the pollution, it wasn't there. He slithered away from all responsibility like a snake.

Lee's rowing was sure and fast. It was no longer necessary to hide, for McGrew and Taters were far behind them. May sat up, took the other oar and began to help with the rowing. She pulled up a blanket from the bottom of the canoe and wrapped it around her shoulders to keep off the rain which had started again.

She was envious of Lee's soft deerskin shirt with the even cut fringes around the bottom. It must be waterproof. The feather on his head was from an eagle and it too could withstand the rain. There was a stately look about Lee in these clothes. He had the same poise and regal bearing as the ghostly Indian Chief.

"What happened to you, May?" Lee asked worriedly.

It was a relief to talk freely. She told about Emily and her friendship with the Indians. . . about the kidnapping, the rough shantyboys and the cruelty of McGrew. . . about her job with Taters O'Toole and his kindness. When she came to describe the vast acres of tree stumps, tears rolled down her cheeks.

"Most of the loggers and owners of the camps don't care at all about the land and the forests," May sobbed. "I'm sure they're destroying the Indian villages and hunting grounds forever."

May caught herself. She was defending the Indians as if she was one of them.

Lee didn't speak. But the deep, cutting thrusts of his paddle were expression enough of an anger that he couldn't put into words.

He was paddling now toward the mouth of the river, toward busy Singapore. May hoped she wouldn't be noticed by any of the shantyboys from the logging camp, but it would be fun to see Emily again. Lee hugged the shore briefly, then docked the canoe beside a large empty schooner.

"I thought you might like to look at the town again, May," Lee said. "We won't be back for a long time. . . . I came here twice looking for you."

May was fascinated and surprised. The rain had stopped and the long board sidewalk along the river front was filled with an amazingly colourful medley of people. There were many, many more buildings and houses than when she and Lee had first arrived.

This was a growing, busier Singapore than she had seen only a few days ago. May was confused. Had years passed by instead of days? Time seemed to be marching ahead in giant strides, without connection to calendars or clocks.

Carpenters, loggers, lumbermen, house joiners, ship builders, storekeepers, traders, Indians, women in elegant clothes and feathered hats and women in long homespun skirts and shawls tending their children passed in front of May's startled gaze, their clothes identifying their professions.

The store was large and bursting with goods. There were stoves, panes of glass, barrels of beans, dried apples, crackers and kegs of honey visible from the dock. And near the store was a blacksmith shop, a wagon and chair factory and a tannery. A small building that squeezed between them had BANK printed in large letters on its front.

"You should see the money the bank makes for itself," Lee said. "It looks like it's worth a million dollars, with Singapore printed across the front of each bill and drawings of ships and fancy ladies around the edges. Lee smiled with some smugness as he added, "Outside Singapore the bills aren't worth a penny."

"Look at the Boarding House," May cried. "It's more polished and fixed-up than it was the day we arrived!"

"They call it the Astor House now," Lee said cynically. "They say in the town that it's the finest hotel around. On Saturday nights there are dances in the dining-room with a fiddler."

"Let's walk through the town, Lee?" May pleaded. "You're dressed like a real Indian now, and I'll keep this blanket wrapped around me."

"No!" Lee suddenly became severe as though he'd been caught off duty. "We're expected in my great-grandfather's village tonight. We must hurry."

May was taken aback. Great-grandfather? Who was Lee talking about? Was the ghostly Chief Pokagon really so closely related to Lee?

Hurriedly Lee lifted his paddle and shoved the canoe away from shore. It glided swiftly down the Kalamazoo toward the old harbour that elbowed in a sharp curve to the Lake. In May's world with Aunt Nell and Uncle Steve the new harbour cut straight to the Lake from "buried" Singapore.

13

Giant pines, oaks, maples and birches stood near the shoreline as though anchoring the earth and supporting the sky.

Lee had become strange and distant. He rowed with added speed and strength and there was a calmness and purpose about his movements that surprised May. When he spoke, it was quietly and with a slow rhythm that she had never heard him use before.

"In Chief Pokagon's village," he said, not turning around, "they call me Golden Carp of the Potawatomi fish totem."

"Golden Carp!" May exclaimed. "That's a beautiful name."

"You are from the Thunderbird clan," he added. "They should give you one of the clan's sacred names, but they will call you May Apple because I told them your story."

May wanted to object. Why should he talk so intimately about her to strangers?

Lee rowed faster and his voice picked up excitement with the speed of the paddle.

"There is a widow in the village whose name is White Gull. She is the exact image of you. When I see her it is as though I'm looking into a clear lake and seeing your face reflected there. She is your great-great-grandmother, May! And you will live with her in her lodge."

May was confused and astonished. Surely Lee wasn't serious? He bent down, cupped a handful of water from the Lake and drank it. May did the same. He was rowing even faster now.

"I am the great-great-grandson of Chief Pokagon and he has taken me into his lodge and calls me 'grandson'."

"Lee." May couldn't silence her protests. "You are a visitor in Pokagon's village. I think he has brought us here for a reason, but we can't join families because we can't stay. And I'm still not sure about. . . ."

May's words were like drifting wind. Lee didn't hear. He was caught up in some feverish new identity that was ripping his previous one cleanly from him.

"Did you know, May, that the Potawatomi, the Chippewa and the Ottawa were once all members of one tribe, and that long ago they came down from the north in Canada and arrived on the shores of Lake Huron. For many centuries the Potawatomi hunted the lands from the Atlantic to the Mississippi River."

Lee paddled the canoe quickly around a large protruding stone, barely missing it. May watched him skilfully swinging his paddle and bending forward with the finesse and sureness of a Great Lakes Indian. His smooth brown skin matched the glow of the sun and its reflection in the water as it broke out for an instant between the dark rain clouds. May wondered if she also was slipping into another world and another past. She wanted to listen.

Lee's words seemed to come from the forests — the awesome, unspoiled forests.

"The Potawatomi became a separate tribe," he said. "We built a council fire for ourselves. We were called 'Puttawa', the blowing of a fire, and 'mi' the word for nation. We governed ourselves and continued to live in peace with the Chippewa and the Ottawa. Our villages were on the Great Lakes shores and along the banks of the rivers that emptied into them."

Lee swung close to the land but he had forgotten to test the depth of the water and the canoe skidded on the sandy bottom of the Lake. He yanked off his moccasins and jumped into the icy water to pull them to the shore. Then he sat on the bow of the canoe and faced May, looking ashen and fearful.

"It is a terrible time for our people, May. Seven years ago, in 1830, President Jackson signed a removal treaty. It required all Indians in the United States living east of the Mississippi to leave their homes and be relocated in the west in Indian Territory. There are no homes there and no burial grounds, no forests for them to hunt and only a few lakes for them to fish. Their lands are being taken in exchange for the western lands. They don't want to go!"

"I know, Lee." May hugged the blanket around her. "It's terrible. They talked about it at the logging camp. Some of them said, 'The savages must go!' "

"And, May" — the ashen look remained on Lee's face — "Chief Pokagon signed this treaty in the same year in Chicago. He told me how he wept when he deeded all the lands of the Potawatomi to the government. Many of our people have already left with bitter farewells. Some are hiding in the woods. My great-grandfather, Chief Pokagon, prays that his small village will be saved, but now it is the seventh year since the treaty was signed, the year when all of us who are still here must be removed."

"Lee, you said all of *us*." May looked down at her

running shoes and then at the damp muddy legs of her blue jeans. She reached into her pocket and held another Petoskey Stone.

"We can't go West, Lee. We belong here and we have to go back."

Lee looked at her blankly. Not far away a small sassafras tree waved in the wind. May raced to it and broke off one of the branches.

"Look Lee," she cried in desperation, "we saw some sassafras just like this along the shore before we left Singing Sands Beach in Uncle Steve's boat. Remember? They're the same as ours — a mitten-shaped leaf. They haven't changed at all."

Lee didn't react. He had moved into the nineteenth century. May was shocked. Was this what Chief Pokagon wanted? She didn't think so.

She was worried. Soon she would be living in the Indian village with a woman named White Gull. But she must not be swept into this long-ago world like Lee and forget where she came from. It was important to remember where they had entered buried Singapore — and that May Apple tea was somehow the key. She must gather some blossoms and fruit as soon as she found another plant.

May slipped her hand into her blue jeans pocket again and felt the sharp peeling knife. She also felt the Petoskey Stone beside it. This particular piece of fossilized coral from ancient limestone deposits wasn't as smooth as the stone she had given Taters. But the constant grinding and polishing of the Lake water that washed over it had turned it into a collector's gem.

"I must never lose this stone," May said to herself, and checked to be sure there were no holes in her pocket. "Whenever I touch it I'll remember home and the time where Lee and I live."

"Past, present and future" — the words floated through May's head — "Lee and I are lucky to live in two of them. But finally we have to live in our own time whether we like it or not."

14

Without warning another spring storm was upon them, twisting and turning and forming white caps that foamed over the tops of the waves. They rushed against the canoe as though wanting to devour it.

Shaken from his reflections, Lee began to act. He tugged the canoe over the sand and deep into the thick cover of the trees. Then he turned it over and propped the bow up high with a strong branch. Two buffalo robes and a bow and arrow fell out onto the ground. May wrapped her blanket tightly around her; Lee hastily threw one of the big robes over the canoe and spread the other on the ground underneath to make a small shelter. They crawled inside.

"I'm sorry, May." Lee looked at her wet hair and soaked jeans and shirt. "I should have made a shelter straightaway."

May was still adjusting to Lee's Indian clothes. She hadn't noticed the details earlier: as well as the deerskin shirt he also wore a breechclout — a wide piece of buckskin between his legs that was held up by a belt and flapped over it in front and in back to make a short skirt. Bright flattened quills, dyed red, blue and yellow, were laced through holes in the buckskin, making perfect geometric designs. Lee wore deerskin leggings too above his moccasins up to his knees, with more fringes cut along the sides. His dark skin glistened as if grease had been rubbed all over it.

For the first time since arriving in Singapore, May felt her old shyness return. She was dirty, wet and shabby beside Lee in his handsome Indian clothes. But she pushed her feelings aside. She was also hungry, cold and wet and had to do something about it. The three rough days in the logging camp had toughened her to this world of work and few comforts and to the wildness of virgin forests where animals lived so close that their breathing became almost a part of her own.

"We'll start a fire, May." Lee seemed more relaxed and like his old self. He was almost gay. "Gather all the dry limbs and twigs and pine needles you can find."

The giant brown trunks of the forest trees felt magically protective to May and the shedding of their leaves and needles at her feet like generous gifts spread before her.

"I almost feel like thanking the trees, Lee," May said.

Lee smiled. "Chief Pokagon *does* talk to the trees. One day I heard him say to a birch tree, 'To build a canoe, I will have to destroy your life. I am sorry for this.' Then he said to me, 'Lee, the Great Spirit has given us animals and things of the forest to be our helpers. We cannot abuse this privilege. We must take only what we need. Nothing must be wasted.' "

"Well, I agree with that." May was thoughtful as she filled her arms with dry branches. "But just think, Lee, thousands of pioneers are pouring into the country. They're building cities with tall buildings and bridges and ships to carry their goods over the Great Lakes. It all takes so much wood. . . . Yet the loggers have no respect for the forests. Thanking a tree would be a huge joke to them."

Lee didn't answer. May wasn't sure he had listened, for he was bending intently over a small pile of dry wood. He took a pouch that hung from his belt, opened it and pulled out a large shell. As May watched, he opened it carefully. The shell was lined with clay and filled with powdery rotten wood, and glowing from its centre was a pea-sized ember that started the wood smouldering. A small flame flickered. Lee set it gently beneath the wood which they stacked under a cove-like shelter of rocks. It caught on the dead pine needles and crackled into the branches.

"I carried our fire with me." Lee's pride was evident. "Stay near it, May, dry yourself and keep the flame burning."

Lee picked up his bow and arrow. Before him was a feast. Rabbits hopped over the ground, a pigeon swooped from the branches, a fat wild turkey wandered into view, squirrels scampered around tall tree trunks.

Lee stepped noiselessly forward. He lifted the bow, fitted the arrow into the bowstring, drew it back until the flint point almost touched the bow and aimed it for the heart of a large rabbit. It struck and the animal leaped and twisted in the air.

"Oh, no!" May covered her eyes with both hands. Even the sight of a dead mouse in a trap appalled her. Blood trickled from the rabbit's mouth, then it fell back onto the ground and was dead.

"Thank you, rabbit," Lee said softly. "Your strength will be our strength." He lifted it by the hind legs and laid it before May.

"It's a man's work to provide meat," he said proudly. "I will show you how to clean and cook it."

May watched. She was hungry and they might be caught in the storm for hours: they had to eat.

Carefully Lee scraped the skin and fur from the flesh with a sharp stone from his pouch.

"This rabbit fur can line a cradleboard for one of the

village babies," he said, stretching it out and hanging it inside the propped-up canoe. "It will be warm and soft. Give me your sharp knife, May. I can slice the meat faster with it."

May handed it to him. The rabbit flesh was cut in long thin strips. Then Lee cut two green sticks from a nearby basswood tree, hung the strips on the end of them and held them over the fire.

"It's just like a barbeque," May laughed.

Lee looked puzzled as though he had no idea what she was talking about. A new thought struck May. Perhaps Lee was blotting out his former life on purpose because he didn't like it.

The fresh-roasted rabbit was delicious. It did give them strength and May, too, was thankful. They found wild red raspberries and small sweet blueberries, and drank rain water from hollows in the tree limbs and on the ground.

Darkness came to the forest swiftly. The moon, which might have showered its moonbeams through the pine needles, was banished by clouds, although the rain was no longer falling. The little fire glowed warm and comforting as the wild creatures of the forest looked on from the high branches and deep underbrush with their luminous eyes.

May wrapped herself in the buffalo robe beneath the canoe and slept soundly without a dream. Lee rolled himself into the other robe under the rocky shelter beside the fire. He would keep the fire burning through the night and in the morning place another lighted ember in the air-tight shell.

15

A bright sun woke them in the morning. The storm had spent its anger and subsided, leaving the Lake exhausted and at peace.

With few words May and Lee ate more roasted meat and berries for their early breakfast and continued southward in their canoe. The sun rose higher in the sky, finally announcing mid-afternoon when they reached another harbour and turned into what Lee called the St. Joseph River.

The wetness of the rain gave off earth smells of damp moss and decaying leaves. Soon a new smell of burning campfires came strongly with the gentle wind. May's heartbeat quickened for around the next bend was Pokagon's village.

She was both fearful and eager to reach it and meet the Chief whom she felt had brought them here.

All morning as the paddles of the canoe made soft laps in the water, May had tried to prepare herself for the Indian village. How would it look? Would the people accept her?

Lee had told her that there were many Potawatomi villages strung along the rivers and beside the Lake in the spring and summer, and that usually about a hundred people of all ages lived in each. Sometimes they were all of one clan, members of the same family. Sometimes two clans lived together.

"The village is prepared for you, May," Lee said. "I think you should cover yourself with the small blanket."

As they drew near, the smell of smoke was even more pungent. Lee slowed his paddling and drifted toward the shore. He lined up his canoe beside the rows of others anchored there. A short distance from the river was a rude fence of wooden poles. Several ponies nibbled grass in front of it. Through the openings between the poles May could see women breaking up the soil with long sticks and sharp bones to plant a garden. Sturdy, naked children ran laughing among them, shooing away birds and pulling up high weeds. May was glad there was bright sun to warm them.

One small boy peeped through the fence posts. He yelled "Aihi" when he saw them. He and his companions with their dogs raced around from behind the poles and soon a noisy, yipping group of boys and girls and dogs had gathered around May and Lee. Lee greeted them with another "Aihi!" But when they saw May they stared in silence. What sort of Indian girl was this with short hair and shoes that looked like corn husks instead of moccasins?

Near their boat was a group of women pounding dirty clothes on the river bank with wooden paddles. Their dark-skinned, round-faced babies were laced tightly into beaded doeskin wrappers and tucked into cedar cradleboards. Some of the babies hung on their mothers' backs by carrying straps across the mothers' foreheads. Others were hooked to the low branches of the trees. They seemed secure in their tightly bound beds and several slept in their upright positions. The mothers nodded a greeting to Lee and May, but did not stop their work.

As they walked into the village, May noticed that a group of men and older boys were gathered in a treeless plot near the gardens. They were arranging rows of posts into a crib to hold pieces of birchbark for shaping into canoes. They nodded a greeting but did not stop their work either.

Over to May's left, fish were drying on racks above slow-burning fires and deerskin had been stretched on frames in the bright sun. Women stood before the skins rubbing vigorously with rounded stones to soften them.

Two laughing boys were running a race with a small white dog bounding between them. And sitting on a stone was a man of many wrinkles lifting his face upward toward the warmth of the sun.

The deerskin, bark-covered wigwams were close to one another but in no special pattern. They were scattered here and there near the gardens and among the trees and looked like rounded domes of beaver lodges built securely against all storms and seasons.

There were no shouts of welcome for May and Lee, for the older people did not interrupt their jobs. But May did not feel unwelcomed. She walked into the village behind Lee as she would walk into a forest. She felt a harmony here that had not been present in the logging camp. The people, the trees, the river and the Lake seemed intertwined with one another.

As they reached the centre of the village a woman walked from her wigwam toward May. She was tall and slim like many others in the village and held her head high. Her hair was gray and her braids were thick and long with age. She had the same prominent cheekbones as Lee and her eyes were dark and tranquil. She lifted one hand.

"I am White Gull of the Thunderbird Clan," she said.

"You are welcome, May Apple; you will share my lodge. When you are washed and dressed, young Golden Carp can join us for a feast."

May was aware that the woman was not speaking English. It must be the Algonkian language of the Potawatomi. She turned to Lee in astonishment.

"I can understand her."

"Of course," he smiled. "It is the language of our ancestors. You will also find you are able to speak it."

May followed the regal lady through the open door of her wigwam and was pleased by what she saw, for the earth and its generous abundance had been gathered with artistry into the furnishings and smells of White Gull's dwelling.

The wigwam had only one room which was round and secure like a beautifully woven basket turned upside down with a strong frame that was arranged as skilfully as the bones of a skeleton. Young oak saplings, stripped of their bark, had been planted in the sod in a circle and bent to form arches, interlacing at the top with opposite saplings that were bent to meet them. Horizontal rings of branches, lashed around the dwelling, held it securely together and sheets of birchbark and flattened elm bark covered the frame outside.

Mats of muted colours and perfectly measured designs decorated the walls. Baskets of plaited cedar bark and basswood storage bags lined the floor, many of them filled with seeds, corn, dried meat and fish.

Without a word White Gull led May to a bench that circled the side of the walls. It was covered with other mats of cattail rushes and furs, and on top of them was a simple deerskin dress, sewn together at the top and down the sides with a fringe around the bottom. Beside it were deerskin leggings and soft moccasins with flattened quills of bright blue, yellow and red laced into flower designs all over them.

"They're beautiful," May spoke easily in the language of the Potawatomi. She knelt on the floor beside them and rubbed her hand over the soft deerskin.

She knew the clothes were for her and when she turned to White Gull to thank her the stately woman smiled. She took May's hand and led her to the centre of the lodge where heated water steamed in a kettle over a wood-burning fire. She threw fragrant herbs into the water.

"Take off your clothes, May," she said, "and I will scrub you. You are covered with mud."

The water felt pleasant and soothing. It was refreshing to be clean.

"Now you may dress." White Gull pointed to the new clothes.

May dressed quickly, tying her jeans and sweat shirt and running shoes into a bundle and tucking them into a small basket under the bench. She quickly took the Petoskey Stone from her pocket and slipped it into a pouch that hung from a belt on her new dress.

May choked several times from smoke that filled the room, for the central fire had no escape for its smoke but a small hole at the top of the wigwam. Steam from bubbling stew cooking in a large shining brass kettle also filled the room.

May pointed to the kettle with surprise. "It's so modern!"

White Gull beamed with pleasure. "I got it at the Butler Trading Post up river from the new town of Singapore in exchange for my dead husband's buffalo robe."

May almost exclaimed aloud and then quieted her excitement and thought silently. The Butler restaurant was still in Saugatuck on the site of the Indian Trading Post! Uncle Steve had told her about William Butler and his family, the first white settlers in the area whose only neighbours at first had been "friendly Indians". White Gull might have been one of them. Perhaps she had slept on the floor of Emily Morrison's log shanty.

White Gull motioned for May to sit on the thickly spread pine needles and cedar bark mats near the fire. She rubbed thick bear grease into May's hair until it shone like the shimmering wet skin of a seal. With a bone comb she fashioned two short braids and held them in place with a snakeskin band. Quickly she pulled a red cardinal feather from her own headband and tucked it into May's. Then she lifted May to her feet and viewed her critically. She was clearly pleased with her efforts.

"You are a lost member of our family, May. It is good that you have come back to live with your clan and be my grand-daughter. We will live in peace."

May was torn. She wanted to throw her arms about this beautiful woman and call her "grandmother". But should she? In this place and time?

May watched White Gull's smile become radiant and could resist no longer. She burst out impulsively, "I will be your great-grand-daughter, White Gull!"

She thought of Aunt Nell and Uncle Steve. Having a great-grandmother need not change her affection for them. A restlessness inside her quietened and an ache that had been part of all her thoughts about her mother was suddenly gone.

Lee now entered the lodge. He stared at May, then at White Gull, then swung back to May again. "It's as I said. In a pool of water, May, White Gull would be your reflection." His voice was joyful.

They ate from wooden bowls and took what they

wanted from the copper kettle with a wooden ladle. Fresh duck meat bubbled inside with strips of dried squash and beans. Fresh berries and nuts were sprinkled over the stew for flavour and there was hot sassafras tea laced with maple syrup to drink. Sitting crosslegged on the floor they ate from the bowls with their fingers. When they had finished White Gull said,

"It is time soon to begin the spring trip to the Sugaring Camp in the grove of Maples. If the people of our village have to move soon, we will need to take the maple syrup with us."

"White Gull," Lee asked suddenly, "Do you want to move to the West?"

"Is there a choice?" White Gull seemed resigned. "I am too old to hide in the woods."

Lee looked at her eagerly and said, "Yes, I think there is a choice."

May wanted to listen but by now tiredness was wrapping around her like a blanket in the circular warmth of the wigwam. The dying fire had smouldered into gentle embers which were like closing eyes.

White Gull broke off her discussion with Lee.

"My grand-daughter, the day has been long for you." She led May to the bench beside the wall. "Lie under the bear fur and sleep. Tomorrow we will pick green plants and fresh berries."

May crawled under the warmth of a black bear's fur and was soon asleep.

16

The crackling of a fire woke May at dawn. The chilly
wind of an early spring day blew under the deerskin
covering over the door and down from the smoke hole.
But it had not touched May under the warm bear fur.
Outside, a light snow dusted the earth. White Gull was
already dipping food from the boiling kettle into her
wooden bowl and had settled near the fire to eat. She
motioned for May to join her.

They were soon interrupted by women and children
entering the wigwam carrying baskets as well as babies
strapped in cradleboards on their mothers' backs. The
women touched May's new dress and stroked her hair.
They exclaimed over her beauty and how she now
looked like her great-grandmother. A young girl with
long braids and dark curious eyes approached her.

"I am Sun Fish," she said. "We are the same age."

May was pleased to be accepted by them. She pulled a
deerskin blouse over her sleeveless dress for added
warmth and took a basket from the bench to be like the
others, but she stayed close beside White Gull as they
packed pemmican and other dried food for their lunch.

Just when everything seemed ready, they were interrupted by a commotion outside. A young Indian runner,
dressed only in a breechclout and moccasins had dashed
from a path in the forest into the cleared land of the
village and fallen to the ground panting for air. Someone
brought him water in a gourd.

People gathered around him. May spotted Lee among the group and made her way to him.

"He has run from a village in northern Indiana," Lee said. "He left there yesterday to bring us a message. He is a runner for Chief Pokagon."

"Lee," May whispered, "that could be almost a hundred miles."

"He can run that far in one day," Lee answered.

As they waited for the runner to recover, the door of the largest wigwam flapped open and Chief Leopold Pokagon stepped outside. He was easily six feet tall and the mantle of deerskin that he wore was slung under his right arm and clasped over his left shoulder. He had the elegance and stance of a chief.

May gasped. Here was the man with the sad, intelligent eyes who had come to her world in Saugatuck and met her near the city hall. With great daring and magic he had brought her and Lee to his world. The power of his presence overwhelmed May and she was drawn to him with unquestioning acceptance.

"I am a Potawatomi," she said to Lee with pride and quiet emotion, "and Pokagon is my chief too."

By now the young runner had caught his breath. He rose and stood before Chief Pokagon, the tight muscles in his bare legs bulging with strength and he looked directly into the eyes of his chief.

"I have a sad message."

There was quiet in the village and all work stopped. More people gathered around and the children sat cross-legged on the ground. May stood beside Lee. The attention she might have received was focussed instead on the runner, who now began to speak.

"Yesterday I was in the village of Chief Menominee in the Potawatomi lands of northern Indiana. A govern-

ment agent marched in among us surrounded by scores
of his men. He stood before Chief Menominee covered
with guns and swords like a porcupine bristling with
many quills. In a voice like a screech owl's he
demanded that the chief and all his people move at once
to the new lands west of the Mississippi. He said, 'We
have told you this for many months.' ''

The runner paused to look at Chief Pokagon to see if
he should go on. The old chief slowly nodded his head.
May saw that his eyes were weary with sadness.

''Chief Menominee rose from his mat. He crossed one
arm over the other, held his head high and spoke loudly
enough for the earth and the sky to hear.''

The young runner shifted his weight from one leg to
the other, but his arms and neck were taut and stiff.

'' 'I did not sign any treaty that I would sell my land,
and I refuse to move,' Chief Menominee said.

''Then he also said, 'The President of the United
States does not know the truth that I did not sign. If he
knew, he would not drive me by force from my home
and from the graves of our ancestors who have gone to
the Great Spirit. He would not allow your men to treat
me like a dog, if he knew the truth. I am not going to
leave these lands.' ''

The young runner paused. The lines about his mouth
tightened and his eyes became slits of anger. May and
Lee stood near him, captured by his story.

May stood proud and stately in her new Indian
clothes. She was a member of the village now and this
news concerned her too.

Chief Pokagon glanced at her and smiled. Then he
turned back to the runner. The chief's shoulder-length
hair blew softly about his face, for he was without his
usual turban and the rib bone that held it in place.

May and Lee jerked forward. Chief Pokagon's long white hair, waving in the wind, was the white mist that had appeared so often before them at the Appleby Nursery, at Singing Sands Beach and in the town of Saugatuck! Chief Pokagon must have been beckoning to them. A great sadness spoke now through the rivulets of wrinkles that streaked his face. It spoke of a suffering so deep it had no end.

"Tell us the rest of the story," he said to the runner.

The young boy took a long breath and bowed his head.

"Many soldiers, with a general at their head, pushed and shoved among the people in the village until the Black-Robed Father came before them weeping and saying,

" 'Let me assemble my children and speak to them for the last time. Allow me to go with them to visit the little graveyard and hold a final service.'

"The general gave the Catholic priest his consent."

The young runner's eyes filled with tears but he did not weep. He lifted his head and his voice grew strong and defiant.

"But Chief Menominee stood apart from all the others with a dagger raised in his right hand. The soldiers cursed him. Then one of them swung a rope around him and pulled it tight. It was hard for the chief to breathe because they wrapped it around him as though he was a fighting bear. They threw him into a wagon and hauled him from his home. His people followed with whatever goods they could gather."

Words choked in the young man's throat and he found it hard to speak. May felt her heart pounding. She could understand now why Lee had joined this village in spirit and in fact.

May saw Lee reach instinctively for the handle of a

sharp dagger he had added to the pouch and stone knife fastened under his belt. She realized, with a start, that a war party might form to seek revenge and that Lee might join it.

Chief Pokagon nodded to the young man to continue. The runner closed his eyes. "The soldiers set fire to the villagers' homes and possessions. I watched from a hiding-place in the woods. A great flame rose and when it died into smoke there was nothing/left but a black patch of earth."

All the men, women and children in Pokagon's village joined together crying, "Aihi!"

Chief Pokagon lifted his hand and motioned the young runner to enter his lodge.

"We will call a Council meeting," he said for everyone to hear. Then he turned to May.

"Welcome to our village, May Apple — one fruit of goodness surrounded by evil," he said. "When the Council meeting is ended you will come to my lodge with Golden Carp and we will eat together."

He tossed his fur-lined robe about him and bent down to enter his wigwam.

What did he mean by the description of her name — a fruit of goodness surrounded by evil, May wondered.

"Lee, the runner's story is so horrible I don't want to believe it." She grabbed his arm. "The Indians fought so many battles to keep their lands. Don't the homesteaders coming from Europe realize whose lands they are taking? I'm sure some of the pioneers thought the vast lands were without owners."

Lee countered bitterly. "Oh, the government agents and the land speculators know whose land it is all right. And what about the greedy owners of the logging camp you just came from."

May nodded. "I know Chief Menominee signed no

treaty. But, Lee, Chief Pokagon *did* sign the Chicago treaty. You told me about it. He agreed to move west of the Mississippi. I think he knew there was nothing else he could do and that's why he looks so sad."

Lee shook May's hand from his arm. His fingers clasped the dagger in his belt more tightly. There was a hardness about the lines around his mouth that frightened her.

"Chief Pokagon is my great-grandfather," he said proudly. "He has courage and is a brave hunter. He has fought in many wars and he is wise. I will listen to his words at the Council."

Lee hesitated as though debating if he should go on.

"But there is something I should tell you," he whispered. "Can you keep a secret?"

"Yes," May answered solemnly.

"Since I returned, May, I have been talking with the young men in the village." Lee glanced about and then walked with May towards the woods. "Many of them will hide in the forest. They will not be ordered by the troops to march West."

"Do you think that's a good idea?" May whispered.

"But there is another choice," said Lee, ignoring her question. "There are families from your clan and my clan who plan to cross the border secretly into Canada and go to the Chippewa Reserve at Port Sarnia. The Indians there are our brothers and sisters. They will welcome us."

May could tell by the determination on Lee's face where his support lay.

"There will be laws and restrictions on their Reserve," Lee admitted. "But we will still live by the Great Lakes, which we know and understand."

May was worried. Lee was including both of them in

this secret escape. Sarnia was their present-day home but they might never be able to return to their own time above the sands of Singapore.

May couldn't reply because White Gull was walking over to them.

"We must leave," she said "or there will not be enough time for the berry-picking."

"Let's talk later," May called to Lee as she left to join the other women.

17

White Gull's face wore a look of unspeakable sadness.

"Until we leave," she said to May, "the land is still ours to use and to care for. Come, May Apple, there is much for me to teach you about the forest."

Sun Fish, the young girl her age, ran up to her side.

"We will try to forget the runner's terrible tale," she said "when we get to the woods."

But as May looked over the sober faces of the other women she knew that none of them would forget.

Then she thought to herself, Sun Fish will know everything about the berries and plants in the woods. I don't want her to think that I am stupid. I will stay beside my grandmother.

An old man and a young man led the women and children onto a narrow path that went deep into the trees. May followed at the heels of White Gull for the dense forest away from the main paths was strange to her and rather alarming. She jumped at a slithering snake in front of her.

"It's a garter snake, May, a harmless creature. It's secretive and timid and wants to hide from us." White Gull laughed. "It eats insects and so is our helper. I must teach you more about the forest; you have been separated too long from the Indian ways."

How does she know about me? May wondered. How could she possibly know about my time? Yet she is such a wise and beautiful woman — and she is my great-grandmother! May felt a joy so deep it sent a tingling warmth to every part of her body and she knew this Indian woman would stay in her heart and her memory for ever.

As they walked deeper into the forest, wild berries were discovered and baskets were swiftly filled. Sun Fish sat with May on a tree stump to eat some of the berries and they laughed easily together.

A little later May knelt with White Gull in the marshes that were still covered with a crust of snow. They brushed it away to find tender greens. White Gull knew instantly which ones to pick and which to leave untouched. How does she know so much without books? May wondered, thinking of Aunt Nell who would love to be with her now. May watched the Indian women's nimble fingers prying over the forest floor, as much at home there as the slithering garter snake.

"The Great Spirit puts every plant and every animal in the forest for a purpose, May Apple," White Gull said quietly beside her. "You know a great deal, but you must learn the names and uses of every animal in the forest. I will help you."

"I know the trilliums," May cried, touching a fresh white three-petalled blossom. And then she saw the patch of dark-green May Apple plants huddled against the earth like a dwarf's village of open umbrellas. Carefully she lifted one of the leaves and was startled by the breathtaking white of the lone blossom beneath. Swiftly she picked it, along with several others, and put them into the leather pouch beside the small Petoskey Stone.

She was beginning to understand why Lee was closing his mind to a return to their own time. He had found a great-grandfather, a chief who sent his spirits soaring and gave him understanding and pride in being an Indian. She was beginning to feel the same tugging temptation. She slipped her hand into the pouch to grasp the Petoskey Stone. It belonged on the Great Lakes beaches where she lived with Uncle Steve and Aunt Nell and where Lee had come to work for them. She and Lee must be patient until it was clear why Chief Pokagon had summoned them here. But then they *must* return.

The baskets were filled, and the women and children in their soft moccasins made no sound as they walked in single file along a narrow path back to the village.

As they approached it, May noticed for the first time a small wood-frame chapel with a cross on the top as well as several other buildings that bore no resemblance to the wigwams. A few cows were also grazing in a pasture. But the most surprising sight of all was a brightly painted two-wheeled wagon drawn by an ox and a horse. It was parked in front of Pokagon's lodge and sitting on the high seat at the front of it was a rosy-faced man as long and lanky as a string of beans. He was dressed in nothing more than a homespun suit of over-alls and a wide-brimmed hat of straw. His bare feet were propped up before him and he seemed intent on wiggling his bony toes.

"Johnny Appleseed!" The children cried and ran to gather around him. May ran too. She had read stories and sung songs about him since she was a tiny girl.

He smiled and laughed at everyone and then, reaching into a sack behind him, gave handfuls of appleseeds to everyone.

"Plant them in soil that is black and wet," he advised in the language of the Potawatomi. May tucked her seeds into the pouch around her belt. He swung himself from the cart and entered Pokagon's lodge.

"He is a friend of our chief," the children cried, "and he comes each spring with his appleseeds."

At this moment Lee with other men and boys

appeared carrying their bows and arrows and strings of ducks and wild turkeys they had shot. Young boys and their fathers carried nets of fish from the river. Lee greeted May with a warm smile.

The berries and freshly killed fish and fowl were taken to a great central fireplace out of doors where larger metal kettles hung along with others which, although they were made of birchbark, would not burn as long as there was water inside them.

Chief Pokagon strode from his lodge in his sweeping cape to scatter sacred tobacco on the fire. All afternoon and the next day there was work to be done to prepare a feast for those visiting chiefs who had been called by swift runners to the council meeting. May and White Gull, along with the wife and daughters of Chief Pokagon, had been chosen to serve food in Pokagon's lodge.

White Gull showed May how to boil sassafras roots with sweet birch twigs and young strawberry and wintergreen leaves to make tea which they flavoured with maple sugar. The taste had a wild, earthy sweetness.

White Gull also made succotash, cutting fresh meat into small squares and adding dried corn and beans and sunflower seeds to thicken it.

"It is best when the corn is green and just cut from the cob."

She gave May a sip from her wooden spoon. May thought it needed some salt, but quickly realized the Indians had none. All their food was seasoned with maple syrup.

When the council day arrived, one by one the chiefs of other villages began to arrive and enter Pokagon's lodge. One especially caught May's attention. His large left eye, which faced her, was painted with a ring of brilliant red. The look from it was sullen and defiant. A long scar, white against his dark skin, streaked down one nostril of his prominent nose and he was further disfigured by a withered arm that hung limply at his side. His breechclout had no fewer decorations than Chief Pokagon's, but his leather leggings buttoned along the outside had a string of tiny bells beside them that jingled as he walked. His black hair glistened with thick oil and a single lock strung with one feather hung to the middle of his back.

"That is Chief Metea," White Gull explained. "The red eye is to signify his savage nature. But he is good to his people and he is a great orator. He has been loyal to the British for many years." White Gull paused as though wondering if she should tell more. "You should know, May Apple," she finally continued, "that the white man brought whisky to our people. It has destroyed many of us. This chief cannot keep away from the drink. It will kill him." White Gull was angry. "Chief Pokagon says that those who drink it have mouths that smell of the dragon's breath. He forbids traders to bring the firewater into his village. I have seen him seize one of their barrels, break it open and pour it onto the ground. Some of our leaders sign treaties to sell their lands when they are drunk and don't know what they are doing."

As the daylight ended and more chiefs entered Pokagon's lodge, Lee called for May and White Gull to come with food from the large outdoor fire.

May thought she had never seen Lee look so handsome and proud. His red-brown skin had been rubbed with bear grease and he held his head high with the same dignity as his great-grandfather. He wore a beaver hat like Chief Pokagon's and his deerskin shirt was decorated with quills in the design of the Golden Carp.

Inside the lodge, which was three times the size of White Gull's, men sat with their feet drawn in on furs and robes that covered the floor. They ate the food that women passed around to them in wooden bowls. Along with the succotash and tea, was pudding made of pumpkin and squash, wild rice cooked with fish, strips of roasted venison and duck and wild turkey.

In the darkness the council fire in the centre of the room blazed with the spirits of logs sacrificed for the dreams and decisions of chiefs.

The women and girls prepared to leave. But Lee, who sat near the back of the lodge, grabbed May's hand as she passed him.

"Stay with me, May," he whispered in English. "It is important that we hear what they say. If you hide in the shadows near me, they won't know you are here."

Lee continued to hold May's hand and she felt its warmth and the pulse-beat in his fingers against hers. She wondered if they were being drawn into an even more lasting bond than this shared voyage in time.

Warmth flowed from the fire and lit flames in the dark eyes of the circle of men. Chief Pokagon sat higher than the others, his white hair held back with the beaver cap, the chalk-white rib bone protruding through it.

Pokagon took a long pipe and filled it with tobacco from his leather pouch; holding the bowl down and the stem up, he lit it. He closed his eyes, threw his head back with the dignity of a chief and drew in the smoke. The pipe was passed slowly around the circle.

Lifting his head even higher, Pokagon spoke. "Brothers of the many tribes of the Algonkian, the Great Spirit has permitted us to meet in council. The

Manitou of our fathers is now among the oaks, listening
to our words, looking in at our hearts. Wise Indians will
be careful what they say in such a presence, and careful
what they think.

"For many moons we have fought to protect our lands
— first as allies of the French and then as allies of the
British against the Americans. There were more defeats
than victories. We have been forced to sign treaties that
will move us from our homes away from the lands of
the Great Lakes of our ancestors where the spirits speak
to us in the trees and in the waters." Chief Pokagon
looked above the heads of those in the council room as
though searching for the spirits to bring him an answer.

"We are told to go west of the Mississippi where we
are strangers and do not belong. The great Chief
Menominee, a few days ago, was tied by ropes and
taken away — and he did not sign a treaty. His broken
people trailed behind him and their village was
burned."

Chief Metea with the red-painted eye moved forward.
His low receding forehead and long aquiline nose made
the shadow of a hatchet against the wall. He spoke re-
soundingly and with vigour.

"Chief of the Potawatomi, I see the Manitou on the
hunting grounds, on the lakes, on the prairies, in the
trees. His face is seen in the sun at noonday, his eyes in
the stars at night. I hear the Manitou in the thunder. But
the white men have learned to build their villages on the
spots where the Manitou speaks to us and where our
fathers killed the deer. . . . They have learned how to
take our hunting grounds." His voice rose. "They have
given us smallpox and put sores on our bodies. Let them
take away the smallpox and the firewater and the
cutting down of trees."

The red-eyed chief could not be stopped. "We count

the white men every summer," he continued. "They grow as fast as the grass on the prairie. I no longer trust the Great White Feathers in Washington or in Montreal. . . . We must drive the white men into the sea!"

May shuddered. She saw Lee reach for the dagger in his belt. If war were called, Lee would surely go. But Chief Pokagon would have the final speech. She and Lee must wait.

Finally Chief Pokagon drew on his pipe and sat erect and dignified in the circle of chiefs.

"I have fought in many wars," he said. "But the white men continue to come like white pigeons blotting out the sun. We might as well stop a cyclone in its course as beat back these on-marching hordes." He drew his hands over his eyes as though trying to erase the picture he had just drawn.

"War cannot stop their numbers. The United States is becoming a strong and powerful nation. When I signed a treaty with them to sell our lands, it was with my heart bleeding." The Chief paused to look about the room, he saw May and Lee at the back and seemed to approve their presence. He watched them now as he continued.

"The Black Robes of the Catholic church came and gave me courage and I wear this crucifix around my neck. With money I received from the United States government, I have bought land not far from here at Long Lake. My family and members of my tribe will move there soon. We will keep the old ways and will not divide the land for individual ownership. There is no other way. I will try to improve my village by raising cattle, planting corn and making better buildings."

Then Pokagon's eyes flamed, though his voice remained calm.

"I have become a man of peace. But I will fight without guns and without tomahawks. I will fight *with words* against the desecration of our earth, our trees, our land, our rivers and our lakes. The Great Spirit has given us the things of the earth to care for and share.

"If we destroy the earth, we destroy ourselves. We are one with the earth."

May and Lee looked quickly at one another and whispered his last words together.

"If we destroy the earth, we destroy ourselves. We are one with the earth."

After a moment it was May who spoke softly but with great certainty.

"It is a message for our time and our place, Lee."

The council meeting ended in division. Pokagon had presented the way of peace. Metea was committed to war. But a third choice, which Lee had mentioned to May earlier, was not revealed.

18

May felt more and more a part of Pokagon's village in the days that followed the Council Meeting. Sun Fish was teaching her how to dye turkey feather quills with blood root and sumac. They planned to use them to embroider a surprise pair of moccasins for Lee. The two had become friends. One night they danced with other girls in the village around the central fire. May watched her friend's feet and found that she too could keep in step and follow the rhythm of the drums that Lee and other young men were beating. A rhythmic contagion spread from the drum beats to the beating of May's heart, as the dancers and the drummers moved together in a celebration of joy.

Each day White Gull helped May learn the names of plants in the forest and how to identify them. The sun was warmer now on some days and tender leaves were budding on the trees. It was hard to dwell on the fear of removal and the need for her to return "home" with Lee.

One day, however, the wife of Chief Pokagon came to May as she planted corn in the garden. She took May's hand and led her to her husband's lodge, where she sat with May in front of the Chief whose mats and bearskins were piled higher than theirs were.

Chief Pokagon's eyes, May noticed at once, had the same sad, intelligent expression that she had seen in them long ago beside the city hall in Saugatuck.

"You heard my speech at the Council meeting, May Apple," he said. This time he spoke in English and his wife's eyes wandered for she did not understand.

"Yes, I did." May was eager to hear more.

"The time will come very soon for you and Lee to take that message back to your people." Chief Pokagon was solemn and unsmiling. "It will be hard for you, May Apple, but you must not delay too much longer. You should go to the Maple Sugar Harvest to help your great-grandmother and then you should leave."

May rose and stood before the Chief, feeling the full burden of his message on her soul. "I will never forget what you said and I promise to carry your words with me when I return. I will try to leave soon."

Chief Pokagon took a pinch of tobacco between his fingers and threw it into the fire. He gave some to May to do the same.

"We have sealed the promise before the Great Spirit," he said.

May bowed with emotion and then turned, preparing to leave. Pokagon held her back.

"I have profound love for my great-grandson Lee," he said sadly, "but I cannot keep him here. He will not listen if I tell him to leave me. He has courage but he is also strong-willed and stubborn. Take him with you, May Apple. Do not return without him. You must carry my words to your time together."

"I promise," May said with grave commitment and left the lodge.

That afternoon as May helped White Gull with the preparations of food, she could think of nothing but Pokagon's words. White Gull broke into her thoughts saying,

"I have decided to stay with Chief Pokagon on the

land that he has purchased. You will stay with me, May
Apple. You will give me great comfort in my old age."

May was dumbfounded. How could she explain to
this dignified woman, whom she now fully accepted as
her great-grandmother, that she had just taken a sacred
vow to leave?

"I will go with you, Grandmother, to the Maple
Sugaring," May said brightly, hoping to change the
subject.

But the subject was changed by Sun Fish who ran into
their lodge to announce that after the maple sugaring,
many of the villagers planned to hurry to Fort Malden
and Port Sarnia for their annual presents from the
British.

"Why do you do this?" May asked. Sun Fish viewed
her friend with dismay.

"Sometimes, May Apple, you are as clever as a fox
and sometimes you appear as stupid as a sleeping frog.
Don't you know that we are given presents because we
have taken up the tomahawk for many years, whenever
King George required?"

"And what are the presents?" May was too interested
to care if she sounded stupid.

"They are blankets which we cannot make from the
deer," White Gull answered, "and iron kettles which
last longer than the cedar buckets. There is cloth for
shirts, and knives which are sharper than bone. There
are tools for building and sometimes there are guns for
hunting and for war. . . . We have learned to depend on
them." White Gull sighed.

"Now we must finish preparing our food and blankets
for the trip to the Maple Grove tomorrow. Go now, Sun
Fish, and help your own grandmother," she said. The
two girls promised to travel together the next day.

In the evening May met Lee after his return from a day of hunting. She told him about the presents, but he already knew.

"The annual visit for presents is being threatened," he told her. "Indians are now punished if they are caught crossing the border into British territory, though so far the American forces at the border have usually been too few in numbers to catch them. . . . And the British themselves want to cut off the gift-giving."

"Then surely it won't be possible for anyone to escape to the Chippewa Reserve?" May interrupted quickly.

"It is going to happen, May." Lee lowered his voice and looked about to be certain they were alone. "I know what we must do. An old Potawatomi chief, who has his village near Singapore, is taking every member of his village across the border to Port Sarnia. His people are members of both our clans and the Chippewa there will take them in, despite the small size of their Reserve. . . . The chief is pressing claims on the British for long and faithful service to them, so that he can cross the border without difficulty."

May was becoming alarmed but she couldn't stop Lee.

"We will go with them, May. We'll follow the Great Sauk Trail through Michigan and take ponies to help carry our supplies. Then we'll ferry across the St. Clair River to Port Sarnia. If there are too many of us, some will go to another Reserve on Walpole Island nearby. It's an island which stretches like a great fish through the St. Clair River."

"No, Lee," May protested, trying to keep her voice low. "You and I have to return to our own time soon. We have a message now from Chief Pokagon. Don't you remember the water and trees that are dying and the fish that are being poisoned?" May thrust her hand into the leather pouch on her skirt and held the Petoskey Stone and the dried May Apple blossoms.

Lee's body stiffened. He looked away from May toward his canoe anchored near the shore.

"I will never return, May," he shouted. "I don't want to talk about it ever again!" He faced May and his expression softened. "You must go with me, May. We belong together." His look was now one of gentle pleading.

May wanted desperately to respond. She needed Lee too. But she had promised with a solemn oath to return soon and take Lee with her. The words of Chief Pokagon began drumming in her ears — "You must not delay too much longer. You must return with Lee to your true home."

"Tomorrow, Lee, I am going with the women and children to the maple grove." May spoke softly. "We'll be gone for a week, White Gull tells me. When I return, we'll talk again." She reached for Lee's hand and held it firmly. "I don't want to leave you Lee — ever. And that's the truth." Tears came to her eyes. She turned away and ran back toward White Gull's lodge.

When she entered she found that her great-grandmother was almost asleep under her rabbit-skin blanket.

"We must start for the maple sugaring camp early, May Apple," she said sleepily. "In other years this is a time of gaiety and laughter for it means that winter is over and the warm seasons are ahead."

She looked up at May who stood beside her.

"These are troubled times, May Apple," she said. "Today there were rumours that soldiers of the Great White Father in Washington are rounding up all the Potawatomi still in Indiana who are under treaty to

move west. . . . In a few weeks they will be here."
White Gull rose in her bed with set lips. "For those who
go, there must be maple sugar to season and preserve
their food. We hear there are no maple trees in the lands
to the west.

"Those who plan to go into hiding near here must also
be given new supplies," she lamented. "Large amounts
too. This year the sugaring will be hard work, for it will
have to be done quickly and without celebration."

Again there was light snow covering the earth. May saw
it when she woke. Their wigwam door was open and
White Gull with other women was already folding up
dried pemmican and packing it on a sled along with
blankets and other supplies. As on their previous
journey for food, several of the women carried babies
strapped to their backs.

"Get up, Sleeping Frog," Sun Fish shouted entering
White Gull's dome-shaped lodge. May laughed and
joined her friend. They quickly ate together from the
kettle that no longer had a fire beneath it.

It was time to start. The three older men accompany-
ing the group took the lead, while the women and
children with their sleds followed behind. May pulled
White Gull's sled. Again their trail led through small
paths far into the forest. For a time the children ran
ahead laughing and shouting. Several hours passed and
the sun rose bright and warm on May's back. She
trudged ahead doggedly, the sled growing heavier with
each step.

At last the sugar camp appeared in a clearing at the
edge of a tall grove of maple trees. A few bark lodges
stood there from previous years and the women
crowded into them, clearing out piles of dead leaves,
nests of forest creatures and banks of snow. These

lodges would be their home for the sugaring time.

"We can sleep together." Sun Fish smiled at May as she placed her bear fur next to May's in the lodge.

No work was started until one of the men sprinkled sacred tobacco over the ground to honour the spirits of the maple trees. Then two of the men felled several trees and hollowed out their trunks for troughs to hold the raw freshly gathered sap. The women stripped bark from nearby birches, carefully trimming it so the tree would not die. They cut the bark into squares, soaked them in water, then folded the corners up and sewed them in place with other strips of bark. Within a short time thirty sturdy sap buckets were produced.

The men notched the maple trees with their toma-hawks, making V-shaped gashes which directed the sap toward a spout made of elder. May, along with the other women and girls, put a wooden yoke on her shoulders and carried full birchbark buckets from the trees to the long wooden trough near the steady burning fire.

The work was hard and May's shoulders ached. She wondered if she would ever be able to straighten them again.

"Let's race to the fire, May Apple," Sun Fish called from behind her.

May groaned inwardly. She didn't want to tell her new friend she had never carried sap buckets before and that just walking with them was an effort.

Sun Fish, who was strong and high-spirited, raced around May with her buckets swinging through the air. One of them struck May's and the two girls tripped and fell to the ground.

"Aihi!" screamed Sun Fish for the girls were tangled in buckets and splashing sap. They looked at one another and began to laugh.

"Quick, May," the eyes of Sun Fish sparkled. "Hide

the buckets before Grandmother sees them. We'll run to the small lake, hang up our clothes and wipe them clean, then jump into the water and have a bath!''

The water was icy. But to May it felt like a soothing balm. They swam briefly, then scurried onto the shore and into their clothes. With lightning speed they filled their buckets again and were soon at the fire where White Gull was stirring the raw sap cooking in a birch-bark trough over the fire.

That night as May crawled under her bear fur, tired and clean, she thought about her friends in this ''buried'' world. There was Sun Fish, Taters O'Toole, Emily Morrison and Lee, who bridged both worlds. If she could make friends in this century, she could surely make them in her own. Her thoughts went back to the last day of her Sarnia school when she had banged her locker door with anger and refused to be identified as an Indian girl. Now she had no fear of returning to school in the fall, and if the giggling girls taunted her, she would say, ''Yes, I am indeed a Potawatomi Indian and my great-grandmother, White Gull, was a wise and beautiful woman. Many people say I resemble her.''

She was too tired to dwell on the question of how she was going to return soon with Lee. It weighed on her mind like a sharp rock.

In the early morning the delicious fragrance of boiling sap filled the air. May and Sun Fish ran to the large fire where White Gull was stirring more sap. There were flat cakes and maple syrup for breakfast. Then White Gull dipped some of the boiled-down sap into a small blanket of snow. It hardened at once and the children, along with May and Sun Fish, scampered for a piece of it.

At last the day came when White Gull announced that

the syrup had reached the correct thickness. The women began pouring it into a trough, pounding it with wooden paddles until it turned into sugar. Some they poured into wooden moulds and set aside to harden. Much of it was packed in birchbark containers called mococks and stored for future use.

As it grew dark and time for the evening meal, the men started another fire. In the twilight, a thumping beat sounded through the forest, the warning of Indian drums from one of the villages. All talk and laughter ceased and those who knew the meaning of the message threw ashes over the fire. There would be no cooking. They would eat dried pemmican and fresh berries with maple syrup.

For many minutes everyone sat quietly near the dim light of the smouldering embers. Then the tramp of marching feet was heard along the path beside the river. A scout who was sure of foot, cautious as a rabbit and sharp-eyed as a hawk, left them and headed toward the river.

The others remained silent. Even the children made no sound.

19

May knew without asking that the tramping feet were those of troops sent to round up disobedient Potawatomi. If their group was captured they might be sent to the west at once without being allowed to rejoin their families or return to their village for supplies.

Capture would be disastrous for May, for a march across the Mississippi to the prairie lands would cut off her return route to her own century. She thought of leaving and hiding alone in the forest, but decided it would be cowardly. Who would pull White Gull's heavy sled loaded with maple sugar? Her great-grandmother needed her help.

May closed her eyes to shut out every distraction from the sound of marching feet. Were they slowing down? Had they left the river path? There were sounds of swishing branches.

The angry growl of a bear cut through the darkness of evening. May could imagine it rising on its furry haunches and baring its front claws for an attack. Another roar filled the night, this time from a different direction. Could there be two bears? Rifle shots zinged upward and an unearthly growl rumbled close by. The marching feet quickened and soon disappeared into the sand dunes far down the river. The bears stopped growling.

The women and children relaxed and began eating

their cold meal. They mixed fresh syrup with water from the river as a special treat.

The scout appeared suddenly as though he had sprung from the earth. He gave the soft growl of a bear. May joined in the laughter which greeted him and ate her cold food with relish.

Before dawn the next morning, the sleds were packed with heavy containers of maple sugar and the single-file journey back to the village began. Another light snow made the pulling of the sleds easier, but May's back and arms ached relentlessly. There were few rest stops and little merry chatter for the sugaring party knew troops were in the area and it would be unlikely that their scout could trick them again.

At one point a cleared opening in the forest greeted them. Majestic oaks towered in a circle about the enclosure, which afforded a view of the great Lake and the beaches that circled it. Grass, as soft as a blanket, covered the ground. May longed to lie on it.

"This is usually our place for rest and food," White Gull said, standing as tall and straight as the oaks. "But today we must seek the shelter of the pines."

As all of them stood briefly in the open space, a straggling line of horses and people appeared in the distance along one of the beaches. Blue-coated soldiers rode at the head and at the end of the line, the barrels of their rifles glittering in the sunlight. Between them Indian men, women and children stumbled along dejectedly, bent like animals of burden with heavy packs on their backs.

White Gull stifled a cry by clamping both hands over her mouth. The others in the group became stoic and rigid. In the distant line they saw an old man fall and his squaw kneel beside him. She tried lifting him, but he had no strength to help. A soldier galloped out of the line and prodded the woman back to her place with his gun. The man was left unattended on the beach as the line of marchers disappeared.

The scout who could growl like a bear spoke softly. "I will go to him and bring him to our village — whether he is dead or alive."

All nodded their approval and continued on their journey in silence. May was sick with despair. She found it hard to lift one foot after another. Her head reeled and when she closed her eyes something Uncle Steve had once read aloud to her from one of his history books flashed through her mind.

By 1837, the Potawatomi, Ojibwa and Ottawa tribes were either expelled to territories far to the west or restricted to cramped reservations within their ancient homelands.

To May the words seemed as cold as though they were carved in ice. They made no mention of the many people who suffered through the event.

When the sugaring harvesters reached their village at last they were greeted with relief and cautious welcomes. Those who had stayed behind had also heard the marching troops. However, Chief Pokagon met the harvesters and praised them warmly for their many containers of precious sugar.

"We will offer the first portion to the Great Spirit and ask for good health, long life and the safety of us all." Pokagon lifted one of the containers. "Carry a small portion to the graves of your family."

The Chief raised his hand as though in a blessing and as he did so May thought he was motioning her to come to him. She did not want to leave White Gull's side, but felt strangely tugged toward the Chief, as though pulled by some strong, magnetic cord. She felt dizzy again and her eyes would not focus properly. She rubbed them and shook her head but it did not help for as she looked at Pokagon he shifted back and forth in front of her like a reflection floating in a rippling river. Then slowly he straightened out and she saw him as he had first appeared to her in front of the city hall in Saugatuck.

The two of them were again in a swirling wind that enveloped them in a cloud. Words flowed from Chief Pokagon's mouth like echoes in a cave. "BOTH RETURN — turn — turn — AT ONCE — once — once." The words were repeated over and over in the confinement of the cloud.

Gradually the cloud faded and she made her way over to White Gull's lodge. A few moments later Lee was running toward her with anger in his eyes and an urgency about his steps that spoke of danger.

"Have you heard, May?" Lee's voice rose with alarm. "A small band of our people from another village has been captured and they are travelling along the Lake shore heading south." Lee tied a blanket onto his back and adjusted the sharp dagger in his belt. "The soldiers left an old man to die alone beside the path."

May thought of the pathetic line of captives she had watched.

"I saw him, Lee, as we returned from the maple grove. A scout went to rescue him."

"My friends have told me the scout was shot and killed by the soldiers. The old man still lies there." Lee's expression was steely and cold. "I'm going myself to get the old man and the scout's body." He stooped down to adjust his moccasins.

But Pokagon had just said, "Go together — at once — at once." May knew that even if she told Lee of this urgent command, he would not listen. She couldn't let him go alone and risk being captured or even killed.

"I'll go with you, Lee," she said quickly. "Wait until I get a blanket and some pemmican." She started to enter the lodge and then turned back. "I won't tell White Gull. It will only worry her."

20

Lee led the way along a narrow path toward the Lake and May followed closely behind. Both of them had learned to walk quietly and not disturb a leaf or a branch, but Lee's present anger was such that he ignored these precautions and cracked through the underbrush, snapping twigs, bending branches and scattering the underbrush until it blurred their path.

May was worried by Lee's impatient fury. She knew the soldiers were armed with rifles and bayonets and that some of them rode on horseback. How could Lee, with a single dagger, protect either of them?

They trudged along through the thick brush, sometimes losing their trail. Usually if they listened they could hear the steady pounding of waves against the shore and they followed the sound as a guide-line. Then, just as they were approaching the open beach where the old man had fallen, it happened. Too late, Lee realized they had not been stealthy enough in their movements. Three blue-uniformed soldiers, with gold braid lining their coats, stepped from the trees and surrounded them.

''Halt!'' they ordered.

May stopped at once, but Lee drew his dagger and raised it in defiance of all three of them. One of the soldiers lifted his bayonet and knocked the weapon from Lee's hand.

"Tie this boy's arms to his sides with a rope," one soldier with a medal on his chest shouted to the other two. "He could cause trouble."

May watched in horror as one of the men held Lee while the others looped the rope around and around his body until he appeared like a man without arms. Lee twisted, turned and kicked until the officer hit him in the face with the blunt side of his musket. Lee reeled but stood his ground.

The soldiers forced May and Lee to march ahead.

It was almost an hour before they approached the band of Indian people.

There were about twenty of them, May estimated, perhaps three or four families. Several mothers carried babies on their backs and two also held a second small child in their arms.

"The children are sick, Lee," May said softly in the language of the Potawatomi. She was walking close to him now to keep him from falling.

"Don't let the soldiers know we speak or understand English," Lee whispered, also in Potawatomi.

May held her arms out to one of the mothers and took the sick child from her. The woman's eyes were filled with such anguish that May wept. The little girl felt hot; her lips were parched from lack of water.

But the soldiers — five on foot and one on horseback — prodded the group forward. There was no stopping for water or food or to bathe the feverish head of a sick child.

There were old people, too, so bent and broken that their steps were aimless and automatic. When they stumbled off the path, a soldier shoved them back into line with the sharp point of a bayonet.

How can they do this? How can they treat these helpless old people with such cruelty? May moaned inside her head.

The younger Indian men, tight-lipped and covered with bruises, were herded together to keep them from protecting their families. Their eyes were angry and helpless, like Lee's.

The marching went on and on until at last they stopped beside a narrow stream. Scanty rations of dried bread were passed out to the Indian people, but most cupped their hands for water.

May held water in her hands for Lee and then bathed the burning face of the little girl. Slowly she dripped some of the water over the child's lips until she swallowed drop after drop.

Remembering the precious pemmican in her pouch, May broke a piece for Lee, some for each of the mothers, and a small portion for the two children. There was none left for her, but she didn't care.

A shouted order came again from the officer with the medal on his coat: "March!"

They marched through the late afternoon and into the evening until the scant light forced them to stop. Fires were lit near the path but there was no other protection from the cold night air and the blankets that most of the families carried were damp and covered with mud.

May helped Lee sit down. The tightness of the rope was causing his hands to swell and she could see that he was in pain. Perhaps she could rub the rope with a sharp rock until it broke apart? As she felt in her pouch again, hoping to find more pemmican, her fingers touched the blade of a knife. It was the sharp peeling knife from the lumber camp that good-hearted Taters

O'Toole had given her as a parting gift!

May blessed him silently and whispered the good news to Lee.

"Loosen the rope slowly," he whispered back. "We'll keep it wrapped around me until the soldiers are no longer patrolling.

"I must stop being angry with my body, May, and begin to think with my head," Lee whispered, still using Indian words. "The soldiers don't know you and I can understand English. When it's very dark I'll creep near their fire and listen to what they are saying. We must work out an escape for everyone tonight. This is only a small group of captives, but I'm certain we'll soon join another larger group with hundreds of soldiers."

May agreed. The events of history, May knew, took hundreds and hundreds of ill, starved and dejected Indian people west of the Mississippi in the heartless Act of Removal. But for this small group there might be some turning back of the event.

The little girl in her arms slept and May covered both of them with her blanket.

The blackness of night came with clouds covering the moon. Lee slipped from the rope, wound it tightly and hung it over his shoulder.

May dozed off, for sleep offered a respite from the nightmare all about her. There were raspy coughs of the ill and stifled cries of the children. Everyone was cold for the ground had not thawed completely and no one was allowed to gather pine needles for mats. Their constant hunger seemed of no concern to the soldiers who gathered around their blazing fire for an evening meal not shared with any of their prisoners.

Later, during a waking moment, May thought she saw one of the young Indian men douse out the soldiers' fire.

Strange, she thought. She could also detect soft movements of people around her. What could be happening? But she slipped back into sleep.

Then Lee came and sat beside her. "Listen carefully, May," he whispered. "Several of the soldiers left for a nearby town for supplies. I heard them talk about it. They didn't want any of us to know. They left only two soldiers on guard. It was easy with the help of one of the young captives named Crowfoot to cover their mouths, tie them with the rope and hide them in the woods. . . . We didn't harm them any other way."

May's heart began thumping like a drum.

"We're telling everyone not to move their blankets, but to put leaves and branches under them so when the soldiers return they will think we're asleep. . . . Come on, May, carry the child. A scout will lead us through the woods. If we travel all night we can take these people to Pokagon's village. . . . There's no time to lose."

"What about the old man, Lee, who was left on the beach?"

"Crowfoot has gone for him. He will bring him to our village." Lee hurried away.

May clasped the child against her and followed. Soon she could discern a single line of people following a leader into the trees. This time there were no sounds of breaking branches or snapping twigs. There was no sound, either, from the lips of the people now they had hope to take the place of tiredness, hunger and despair.

The night and the path seemed endless to May. Once the group stopped for water and May washed the small girl's face and gave her a drink. The heaviness of her body weighed on May's arms until they felt paralysed. But she was determined not to let go.

On and on they marched. Owls hooted from the trees

in alarm. Larger animals glared at them but did not attack. Once an old woman stumbled from exhaustion but a young man lifted her gently and carried her over his shoulder for a while.

Dawn came slowly and at last May saw the familiar waters of the St. Joseph River and could smell the smoke from an Indian village.

The scout left them and without a sound entered the waking village. Then just as silently, the exhausted people were taken into many different lodges. On the surface it appeared that nothing unusual had happened.

21

May and Lee stood worn out before White Gull's lodge. The fire inside was still unlit.

"Now that our brothers and sisters are taken care of, May, we must leave again," Lee announced with tired urgency. "This time we will take the canoe and can take turns sleeping in it."

Lee's announcement barely registered with May. She was so tired that the thought of sleeping in the bottom of a rocking canoe seemed attractive.

"Why are we going so soon, Lee?" May asked, yawning.

"We must join the old Potawatomi chief near Singapore. His whole village is leaving today for Port Sarnia and the Chippewa Reserve. He is expecting us. If we stay, we may also be pushed west by the soldiers."

Lee paused to acknowledge the silent figure of White Gull who had woken and now appeared beside them, then he turned to May.

"I have talked with Chief Pokagon and he said to me, 'Go at once!' "

May knew this was Pokagon's way of telling Lee "goodbye". Their time in Pokagon's century had run out. He could no longer guide or protect them.

May's eyes met those of White Gull's and she felt deep sadness and an unspoken farewell. May was certain that White Gull knew about Pokagon's command.

Impulsively she flung her arms around her great-grandmother and tried to hold her close, but the warmth of the older woman's body seemed to be receding. Only her eyes and her voice communicated.

"Take this basket," White Gull said. May looked inside. There were her blue jeans, sweat shirt and running shoes and beneath them the clothes that Lee had worn when they entered Singapore. White Gull's voice grew weaker and more distant.

"You must take your memories, May Apple, and my love. You will be brave as your people have been brave and you will have courage as they have had courage. The Great Spirit who created us will not desert you."

A swirl of white mist circled the basket and then drifted over the matching white hair of White Gull's high-lifted head. May knew that Pokagon's spirit was still with them and perhaps it always would be.

"Why don't you come with us, White Gull?" Lee asked.

White Gull shook her head slowly and walked toward her lodge. May looked about frantically for Sun Fish. She could not leave without saying goodbye.

"Sun Fish!" May called as loudly as she could. But the sound of her voice did not carry. It remained static in mid-air.

White Gull spoke as though from a great distance.

"You will find another friend like her, May Apple, in another place and another time."

"Come, May," Lee shouted with impatience.

May walked to the canoe and stepped inside. She saw that Lee had packed it with buffalo robes and dried food, and added her basket of clothes.

At least, she thought, the boat is headed in the right direction.

Lee took his place at the bow and plunged his paddle straight and deep into the water to give them a rapid start. His eyes focussed ahead and he did not look back.

May wrapped herself in a blanket preparing to sleep. But she had to look back. How could she leave her Indian home and her great-grandmother without a final farewell. She turned around and her heart stopped beating. The canoes were gone from the shore. Smoke no longer spiralled from the wigwam fires. The lodges were totally erased. The village was no longer there. Then suddenly a cloud of white mist billowed over the ground and above the trees where the village once stood. It swept silently back and forth with the wind, weaving a pattern of peace and beauty. May did not know how to tell Lee about it so they rode on in silence.

The light canoe skimmed swiftly down the St. Joseph River until they came to the wild, swishing waters of Lake Michigan. A storm was brewing from dark clouds that churned in the sky and the Lake was responding with uneasy ripples.

This time May was prepared for rain, for her deerskin clothes were waterproof as was the hide of the buffalo robe. She felt in her leather pouch to be certain that the May Apple blossoms and the Petoskey Stone were there. Then she tucked the basket of clothes safely beneath the robes at her feet.

When May woke and prepared to give Lee his turn to sleep, she sensed a brooding and warning in the wind that buffeted them. But Lee, sitting straight at the prow, was excited and confident in his single purpose. Wearing a beaver turban with the rib bone of a deer protruding from it, he was an Indian chief helping to lead his people to another hunting ground. In his thoughts, he and the old Potawatomi chief would meet defiantly as they guided an entire village across the blue waters of the river St. Clair to Port Sarnia. They would follow the connecting waterway that led from one Great Lake into another and so would remain on a small piece of their ancient hunting grounds.

The canoe curved into the emptying mouth of the Kalamazoo River. The strength of the current caught them both by surprise. They tugged with effort to paddle upstream and around the oxbow curve to Singapore.

"We won't stop in Singapore," Lee shouted back to May. "We'll travel along the opposite shore again to miss the floating logs. I'll take my rest later."

But we have to stop in Singapore, May thought in desperation.

Lee laughed, his mood cheerful. "If we see Cook O'Toole, he won't know you in your Indian dress."

Their boat hit a sharp rock and swung onto a sandy beach. Lee jumped out to keep it from tipping. May followed him.

"Look, Lee," said May, pleased by the forced landing, "here are fresh green sassafras sprouts. I'll pull up the roots to boil for tea." She checked again on the May Apple blossoms in her pouch.

"There isn't enough time, May," Lee said. He quickly inspected the canoe for damage then said abruptly, "Get inside," and pushed the canoe again into the water. "Finding the sassafras is no big deal. There will be plenty all along the way."

"O.K.," May answered. They still had to round the curve in the river before reaching Singapore. She was amazed that they both seemed to have lapsed into the informal English of their own time.

As they drew closer to Singapore, May grew uneasy.

"You'd think we would hear the sawmills by now, Lee," she called out. The wind had lessened as they left the big Lake and moved inland.

"Maybe they've closed the mills for some sort of holiday," Lee shouted back. He paddled faster, staying close to the shore opposite the town.

They turned the final bend and looked ahead. Then their oars froze for a moment in the air.

On both sides of the Kalamazoo River, where the giant virgin forests of white pine had stood for centuries, were rows and rows of tree stumps half buried in the drifting sand. Stripped of their anchoring trees, the sand dunes had begun to shift with the ever-blowing winds.

The white mist appeared unexpectedly, twisting angrily around the useless stumps.

"They have destroyed the earth. Singapore is being buried under the sand!" Lee whispered in anguish, for the desecration brought with it the hush of a vast graveyard.

22

Before swinging their canoe around the oxbow bend of the Kalamazoo River both May and Lee had expected to find Singapore growing even faster than when they had seen it on their trip to Pokagon's village. They had anticipated finding tugboats, fishing boats and sloops tied to the docks and three-masted schooners being loaded with boards.

White Gull, who had been to Singapore only a few weeks before — at least May thought it was only a few weeks — to trade furs at the Trading Post, had told May with astonished eyes about the twenty-three buildings along the shore line, the sidewalks made of boards that stretched along the river front, the new and larger lumber mill, the finely dressed ladies and gentlemen walking in and out of the great boarding house.

They had both thought the river would be so jammed with logs that they might have to carry their canoe upstream for a distance to avoid them.

Now — the view of Singapore was blank devastation. There was nothing in front of the once-busy town but a solitary sloop with a bent mast and a torn sail swinging ghost-like from a battered mooring.

"Maybe we came up the wrong river, May?" said Lee as he paddled across towards the sloop.

"No, Lee. This is where Singapore was."

May realized what was happening: their time in the past was running out and they were now seeing events in a fast-changing kaleidoscope. Her face paled as she pointed beyond the shore where the sawmills had been, to the site of the Boarding House. Only the top gables of the huge building rose above the yellow sea of blowing sand.

"They have destroyed the earth, Lee. People's greed has destroyed a whole town."

"Look, May." Lee pointed to a building with the top floor still visible. Sand sifted through the windows and piled in drifts around the chimney. The windows gaped at them as though struggling for breath against the stranglehold of sand. A few juniper bushes grew beside the house, like prickly porcupines clinging on with feisty courage. Several jack pines remained, unwanted and scrawny. Here and there old boards stuck out from the beaches; the boards and some pilings in the water with mounds of sawdust between them seemed to be all that was left of the city that settlers said would someday equal Detroit and Chicago.

May hoped that Lee was beginning to understand what was happening. He had rooted himself so completely in Pokagon's village and in Pokagon's time. He had been so determined to remain there. . . .

"I don't want to stay here!" Lee turned back toward the canoe. "The town deserved to be destroyed." He rubbed his hand gently over the quill design of the Golden Carp on his deerskin shirt, then stepped into the canoe. "We must hurry up river to the village of the old Potawatomi chief. If he's started for Port Sarnia without us, then we'll follow. Come along, May."

May was shaken. Didn't Lee understand what was

taking place? Hadn't he seen the destruction of Singapore with his own eyes? Was he blind?

She grabbed Lee's sleeve.

"Wait, Lee, it's getting colder and I'm hungry. We can boil some tea and eat our pemmican here."

"Not in this dead town. It's creeping with skeletons." Lee was adamant.

May was desperate. Should she refuse to go and trust Lee would stay with her? She couldn't risk his leaving in the canoe alone.

"Ahoy!" a loud rasping voice called from the top floor of the only house still visible in Singapore, the house with the gaping windows. A thin arm waved to them out of one of those windows.

Before May or Lee could answer, the man opened the window and stepped out of it. He slid down the sand bank to the beach and walked towards them.

"Speak English?" he asked, standing up and brushing the sand from his ragged clothes.

They nodded. May pitied the man. He looked as deserted as the buried city; thin and scrawny with pants as worn and tattered as the sail on his sloop near their canoe. His large eyes were red-rimmed and bloodshot from the blowing sand and his gray hair had a sandy yellow tinge.

"Ain't been no one stopping here for months — Indians or whites." He held out a grubby hand. "My name is Jim — Jim Nichols." May shook it gingerly.

"What happened to Singapore?" She was unable to think of anything else to say.

He swept his thin arm over the banks of the river and the shameful stubble of tree trunks.

"See for yourself. The loggers and the sawmill owners thought the trees would last forever." He paused to rub sand from his sore eyes. "Why, the pine forest was so thick along these banks when I was a boy that you couldn't see the river."

He looked more closely at their deerskin clothes.

"When I was young I used to play with Indian boys and girls dressed just like you. They camped and fished along the river every summer — right up there." He pointed to the opposite shore. "They bathed their babies every morning in that little inlet where the water was still and warm."

Lee tugged May's arm impatiently.

"We're sorry about your town," he said abruptly to the man, "but we're on a journey and we have to hurry."

The old man looked at Lee quizzically and then his face beamed with a wide smile.

"Why, young man," he said with delighted surprise. "You're the image of the famous Chief Leopold Pokagon who used to visit these parts when I was a boy. He was as tall as you but his hair was white. He could speak English as well as any white man — in fact as well as you."

Lee became rigid.

The kaleidoscope was spinning rapidly now, May knew. In another hour this man might vanish and another generation would walk along these beaches. Maybe soon it would be 1906 when the new channel was cut for the Kalamazoo to flow directly into the lake from the spot where they were standing. Chief Pokagon had said "Go at once." They couldn't wait.

May could feel Lee's pain. He had found a better home and a better identity in spite of the historic Indian Removal Act. And now, with all his bravery and courage, his passion to lead his people across the border, the passage of time was robbing him of being a living part of the journey.

Cautiously Lee asked a question of the ragged man.

"Have you seen Chief Pokagon recently? Was he here last week or even the week before?"

Astonishment circled the old man's open mouth.

"Why, lad." He shook his head. "The good chief's been gone some thirty years. If I remember right he died in 1841."

Lee threw both hands over his face and turned his back to May and the old man, who didn't appear to notice. The fact of Chief Pokagon's death was the last straw. Now Lee could no longer hide from the fast-changing scenes. There was nothing he could do to stop them. His body shook but he did not cry.

"With the forests gone," the lonely man rambled on, "the mills were forced to move and the people left right along with them. The bank, the stores, the trading post all closed. The harbour filled up with sand and the lake schooners couldn't bring in the mail and supplies any longer. The houses were deserted. I'm the only one left. The sand buried us. With the trees gone, there ain't nothing to hold it down any more. He wiped his watery eyes with the back of his hand.

May took Lee's hand gently and started walking up a sandy slope to the protruding gables of the Boarding House.

She turned back to the man.

"I think we'll build a fire to boil some tea." She handed him a small package of pemmican. "The Indians probably gave you some of this when you were a little boy."

He nodded and tucked it in his bulging pocket, then handed her a box of matches.

"I'm going up the river to catch some fish for supper. If you're here when I get back, I'll share them with you."

As he trudged off into the distance both he and his sloop slowly evaporated into the sea of sand.

May quickly gathered twigs and broken branches and placed them in a circle of stone. The matches were a godsend for, without them, starting a fire could have delayed them another hour. It was important to boil the tea quickly and that she and Lee both drink it at the same time.

She had carried the basket of jeans and running shoes with her when she left the canoe and when she opened it she found more pemmican tucked at the bottom as well as a small copper kettle. White Gull had put them there, and she felt a surge of affection for her loving and thoughtful great-grandmother.

May lit the twigs and dried leaves and started a small fire. A spring close by provided water for the kettle, which she hung on a bent green limb over the now blazing fire. She quickly broke the fresh sassafras twigs into small pieces and stuffed them with all the dried May Apple blossoms into the kettle. She slipped the Petoskey Stone into her blue jeans pocket.

Lee said nothing. He stood near the exposed gable of the Boarding House, rubbing his fingers over the weathered boards. His eyes drifted down to the canoe that was anchored alone now along the river. A chill wind blew off the lake, rippling the river water and sparking the fire that glowed under the kettle. The water bubbled inside.

"I have to go up the river in the canoe, May. Maybe things haven't changed as much there." Lee spoke in a strange, muffled voice. "You wait for me here."

May froze. She *had* to keep Lee here. She tried to remain calm.

"How about a drink of hot tea first. It's getting cold again."

"Well, all right, but hurry." Lee held out his hand and took the filled gourd.

May crossed her fingers for good luck.

They drank at the same time. The taste was both sweet and bitter and the fragrance coming from the steaming cups floated back and forth before May like the sleepy rhythm of a swinging hammock.

"We must change clothes!" May realized with alarm and, quickly taking hers from the basket, walked to the other side of the gable and pulled them on. She carefully folded the soft deerskin dress and leggings, hugged them to her for a moment, and then buried them in the sand.

"Lee." It was an effort for May to call out his name. "Here — are — your — clothes." She spoke each word slowly. "Put them on. We — are — going — home."

Lee barely opened his eyes. He moved in jerks, pulling on his sweat shirt and jeans and carefully folding the deerskin clothes of a young Potawatomi chief. With May's help he, too, buried them in the sand.

They drank again. Suddenly the sky above them became splattered with bits and pieces of colour from the kaleidoscope that shifted and turned in rapidly different patterns. Around and through the colours in almost joyful abandon circled the familiar white mist like a spinning top.

A singular funnel-like wind roared up from the beach suctioning in the colours and the mist along with May and Lee, pulling them into its vortex. The funnel began to spin — slowly at first, then faster and faster. It

gathered sand and rocks and bits of limbs and trees with
May and Lee in the middle. Then it barrelled up and up
and up through layers of sand, hitting the air with an
explosion that threw May and Lee onto a sandy beach.
They gasped for air and their fingers dug into the sand.

An old man with a snake-like cane strode back and
forth in front of them, and not far away, anchored to a
pier projecting into a river, was a motor boat with
''Appleby Nursery'' printed on its side. It bobbed up
and down on rough waves that were rolling in from
Lake Michigan.

''It's been a bad storm,'' the pinched little man said in
a matter-of-fact way as though their appearance was not
at all unusual, ''but it didn't wash away the pollution. It
still smells rotten. You know, I thought the two of you
had drowned in the river. Mr. Appleby's been looking
for you all night and he's mighty worried.''

23

"Uncle Steve has looked for us all night?" May mumbled the pinched man's words aloud, trying to focus on their meaning and on the scene before her.

She and Lee were standing on a wide sandy beach. Their bodies were no longer spinning, but May's mind was still in a whirl. The river banks that, for them, moments before, had been a desolate field of tree stumps were again the familiar high dunes anchored here and there with beach grass, some juniper bushes and a scattering of cottonwoods, maples, oaks and sassafras. May decided to think backwards. She had made tea with May Apple blossoms and sassafras. And the tea had been the key to their return.

Return? Of course, they had returned! They were on the Kalamazoo River near Singing Sands Beach with buried Singapore beneath their feet.

"Aunt Nell! Uncle Steve!" May cried out, wanting desperately to see them.

"I told you," the sour-faced little man said, shaking out a rain hat and pulling it over his small head. "Your Uncle is looking for you."

"Where is he?" May cried. "Which way did he go?"

"I didn't watch." The man was uninterested as well as angry. "All I see around here are dead fish and dirty, stinking water." He smashed his cane into the sand and cracked it. The snake head on the handle drooped.

The cane reminded May of the trees she and Lee had planted in front of his house.

"Are the trees we planted still standing?" she asked.

"Yes, they stood up in the storm fine, just fine," he scowled. "I may order some more to hold down this bloomin' sand." He kicked at the skeleton of a fish. The beach was littered with rows of dead or dying fish. "Or maybe I'll just sell this place and move away from this stinking pollution."

"No one will buy a house on a polluted beach," May answered simply. "The people who live around here are going to have to work together to find out what's causing it."

"Hrumph." The man glowered at her.

May wondered that she could speak so freely. She would never have opened her mouth in front of this man before. She turned to Lee for some response. His eyes were vacant and he was standing stiff and inert, as though frozen. The warmth of the sun had no effect on him.

The old man pulled away from the two of them as though frightened.

"Something is wrong with your Indian friend there," he said to May. "He looks like he's been hit on the head by a rock." He moved farther away from them. "Another thing, I didn't notice you were wearing moccasins when you planted those trees yesterday afternoon."

May looked down at her feet and then at Lee's. It was true. They had left their deerskin clothes in Singapore but had forgotten to leave the moccasins. She quickly took hers off and tucked them under her arm.

The old man with the cracked snake cane had talked about "yesterday afternoon". They had only been gone from here during the overnight storm. Even so, Uncle Steve and Aunt Nell must be frantic. She tried to call out to the man for more information, but he had shuffled off into his home behind the newly planted pines.

"Lee!" May tried shaking him. Surely the effects of the May Apple tea had worn off by now? He didn't move. His eyes stared down at the moccasins.

That must be it, she decided. He's still connected with Pokagon's time through the moccasins. They can't have had the same effect on me.

She took Lee's hand and led him to the motorboat. The water was quieter now and the motor boat almost motionless. Lee stepped over the side and sat with a jerky movement beside the motor. May bent down quickly and pulled off the moccasins, hiding them behind her. The effect on Lee was electric. He blinked with startled disbelief, like someone waking from a nightmare.

"We're back, May, on the Kalamazoo River." He rubbed both hands over his sweat shirt and blue jeans and stared at his bare feet. "It didn't happen." He was bewildered. "It was just a dream." He looked along the banks of the river, now also polluted by refuse from Singing Sands Beach.

"You were in my dream, May." Lee faced her, his eyes as troubled as the swill-washed water around them.

May understood. If Lee thought that Chief Pokagon and White Gull were only a dream it would rob both of them of the respect, pride and joy in their Indian people they had gained.

May shoved the moccasins in front of Lee.

"It wasn't a dream," she said solemnly. "You were there and I was with you, and Chief Pokagon gave us both a message to bring back to our own times. These moccasins were given to us in his village!" She held both pairs in front of her.

Lee grabbed May's hands and the moccasins with them. He was extraordinarily excited.

"May," he said breathlessly, "I wanted to march to Port Sarnia with our people over the Old Sauk Trail and across the St. Clair River to the Chippewa Reserve. They did make it, you know. We wouldn't be living in Sarnia today if they hadn't. And Chief Pokagon did build another village in Michigan. I've read about it." He almost laughed with relief.

"Princess! Lee!" A cry came from a slovenly dressed man approaching them from up river. He ran toward them with awkward, ponderous strides. Uncle Steve. He rushed to May and grabbed her in his arms. As he did so, May saw Lee stuff the moccasins inside his sweat shirt.

Uncle Steve wept and laughed at the same time.

"It was a terrible storm," he babbled. "Two fishermen and their boats were pulled out into the Lake by the undertow. They haven't found them yet. . . . I've been out in the storm all night looking for you. We alerted the coast guard and Aunt Nell drove to Saugatuck to tell the police. . . . You're alive, Princess; you're not even hurt."

May laughed. "Lee took care of me, Uncle Steve. He tipped over a boat and we crawled under it. You should thank him."

Uncle Steve grabbed Lee's hand.

"Lee, Lee," he babbled again. "How can I ever thank you?"

Lee smiled. "Get in the boat. I think I can start the motor. The two of you scoop out the water in the bot-

tom. We'd better go straight back to the Nursery and
Aunt Nell.''

The boat rode easily over the now calm but murky
Lake and their motorboat soon docked near the
Nursery. Aunt Nell saw them coming and stumbled
down to meet them. Her tight blue jeans were soaked
and mud-stained and her hair was a matted bird's nest,
but the smile on her face was sunshine.

Before late supper at the Nursery that night there was
a simple prayer of thanksgiving and May felt no confusion in her mind or heart over any difference between
the God that Uncle Steve thanked for their safe return
and the Great Spirit of her great-great-grandmother,
White Gull.

Work at the Nursery began early in the morning. Window panes had been shattered by the winds and needed
replacing. Flowers, plants and trees had been uprooted
and demanded rapid replanting. May and Lee were
relieved to be busy and to be free from too many questions about their survival in the storm. Only once when
they were in the potting shed alone did they have a
chance to talk about Singapore.

"What did you do with the moccasins?" May asked.

"When I started to take them out of my sweat shirt
last night, there was nothing there but a little dust and a
few broken quills." Lee carefully unfolded a handker-
chief in which he had wrapped the quills. The dye had
worn off and they were colourless. May touched them
gently. She took one of them, wrapped it in some moss,
tucked it into a small box and put it in her pocket next to
the Petoskey Stone.

"The moccasins didn't belong in this century," Lee
admitted.

Wreckage caused by the storm brought customers and

phone calls to the Appleby Nursery. Their demands and questions were endless:

"Our newly planted White Pine has been uprooted. Could you please send someone to replant it properly before it dies?"

"How can we save our ancient oak that has splintered along its side?"

"We need a dozen Ponderosa pines for a windbreak against future storms. Rush, please."

Aunt Nell, as the general, monitored the calls. Uncle Steve gave May and Lee instructions and sent them off in the pick-up truck loaded with trees, packages of manure, varieties of mulch to enrich the soil, shovels, ropes and saws. On the difficult cases he went along himself.

May and Lee worked steadily and with precision. Each day's end found them exhausted but satisfied. There was no talk of "lazy Indians".

"I think Chief Pokagon would approve." Lee smiled at May as he shovelled black dirt around a newly planted oak while May held the tender trunk up toward the sky.

"I learned so much from White Gull that I can use at the Nursery," May answered wiping perspiration from her forehead.

There was little time for visits to the Lake. For a few days residents around Singing Sands Beach were hopeful that the churning waves of the storm would have buried the pollution, but once the storm's wreckage had been mended, a cry for help came from everyone in the area. The increasing problem of the dead fish and water pollution hung over all like an invasion.

"We have to do something, May." Lee's hands

tightened around his belt as he and May took time off from their work to walk along the cluttered beach.

"I know," May added, "Chief Pokagon meant us to."

That evening Uncle Steve and Aunt Nell announced that they planned to go to a meeting called by the Young Environmentalists in a disused warehouse about a mile down their road.

"I've been talking to people," Uncle Steve said. "The pollution's worse than we thought. We can't just sit around and hope it will go away."

"I want to go too," May said quickly.

"All right," said Lee. "Why don't I drive us there in the pick-up truck?"

As they drove away from Singing Sands Beach there were hopeful smells of spring along the road from budding lilacs and blooming apple blossoms. May had noticed that the trees along the beach had no buds at all. Even here the pollution hung in the air like thick, sour scum.

The yard outside the meeting house was jammed with cars. Angry and muttering people were swarming about like disturbed bees over an upturned hive.

Lee swung the pick-up truck into an open field near the building and the four of them elbowed their way to a bench near the front of the meeting-room. A makeshift stage had been erected, with a loudspeaker system. Lights went on. Outside were blinking red flashes from police cars which roamed back and forth directing traffic.

A young boy beside May pointed at her and said to his father, "That girl and her boy-friend look like they're Indians."

His father glanced up.

"Wonder what *they're* doing here," he muttered. "Hope it doesn't mean trouble."

Lee leaned down and whispered in May's ear, "You have to learn not to listen to those kind of people."

May wasn't sure.

A young man rose behind the microphone and a spot light flashed over his face. He was thin with unruly black hair and a serious, no-nonsense look. He wore thick glasses, a gray sweat shirt and patched blue jeans.

"I'm president of a volunteer organization called the Young Environmentalists." He spoke firmly without drama. "Most of us are studying the environment at the university, but we've decided to take time off from our classes to do something about the pollution of the Lake. We can't let Singing Sands Beach just die."

There was some slight applause. "We've signed a pledge that we will save and defend from waste the natural resources of our country — its soil, its minerals and wildlife, its forests and water." He paused. "We are going to try to co-operate with all the government authorities on this matter. But we plan to watch them and make certain that every problem is investigated."

May and Lee listened tensely.

Speaking carefully and plainly, he talked of needing new waste-water treatment plants, of not letting chemical poisons seep into the water above and under the ground. He talked about unchecked hot water discharged into the Lake from nuclear and other plants which could kill thousands of fish. He talked of the tons of pollution pumped into the air from factories and automobile engines and the resulting acid rain that had already killed trees and animal life in and around many rivers and lakes.

"Those American and Canadian lakes are now dead," he said.

"The problems are enormous," he went on, spreading his arms wide. "We don't know which ones relate to our problem here, but when we find out we can solve them. We have studied them and *we know what to do!*"

A middle-aged man, smoothly dressed in a suit of summer seersucker, walked with authority and assurance to the platform. His smile appeared calm, but his flushed cheeks belied frustration.

"Let's not get too alarmed about all of this." His voice was as smooth as his dress. "I've lived in this area all my life. Things go up and down. One year there are dead fish and the next year there aren't." He glanced at the young president of the new organization and there was a look of intolerance in his eyes. "Some of our young people get over-dramatic. It's better to learn from those of us who have some years of experience."

"That's right," a fat man and his wife who sat apart from the others in the room nodded. "We don't want a bunch of young radicals running our beach."

A pert lady with clipped brown hair stood up and snapped at the speaker. "It's fine to remain calm and pretend that nothing is wrong. But you have no plan. You just want to wait and wait and wait. Could it be that you are hiding something, Mr. Struthers?"

The young president intervened. "Let's try not to get personal," he begged. "We are here to solve a community problem together. Are there others who would like to say something?"

There were mumbles here and there.

"We want action now. We don't want a lot of study."

Another voice grumbled, "Get rid of the dead fish. We'll sue if the Lake keeps smelling like a garbage dump."

Most of the people, however, were serious and were listening.

Without anyone noticing Lee and May walked quietly to the platform. They both stood tall and unafraid beside the president.

''We want to say something,'' Lee said and took the microphone in his hand.

24

The silence of the audience was like the suspense before the shooting of a deer in the hunting season. Uncle Steve and Aunt Nell looked stunned.

May felt a tingling shiver run down her back. She looked to Lee for courage. His dark skin had a golden, reddish hue in the spotlight, his narrow eyes were as direct as two perfectly crafted arrows. She felt proud to be standing beside him.

Lee spoke slowly without raising his voice.

"Before the white man came to live in Michigan," he said, "our Indian tribe, the Potawatomi were in complete possession of all the lands surrounding the lower part of Lake Michigan. One of our chiefs, Leopold Pokagon, who was my great-great-grandfather, sometimes left his Indian village to walk the streets of Saugatuck and of the city of Singapore that is buried now under the sand." He paused to wipe perspiration from his head with a red bandana from the pocket of his jeans. The only sound in the room was the muffled sneeze of a child.

"Chief Pokagon could speak English and he was respected. A lodge and a park and a town were named after him."

No one in the audience moved. A past, which was as buried in their minds as the forgotten city of Singapore, was being unearthed in the darkened warehouse.

May noticed that Lee was looking now far over the heads of the audience. He had almost forgotten them, but he didn't stop talking.

"The white man came to Michigan in larger and larger numbers. They took away the Potawatomi hunting grounds. They gave us small-pox and many died. They gave us alcohol so that we couldn't think and they cut down our virgin forests." Lee did not sound angry — just sad. "In that time," he continued, "the waters around Singing Sands Beach were not polluted. The water was so clean and pure you could make a cup with your hands and drink it."

May closed her eyes. She was back in the village of Chief Pokagon on the banks of the St. Joseph River. The Council was meeting and Chief Pokagon was speaking . . . except that when she opened her eyes the speaker was Lee.

He talked about the Indian Removal Act and told how Chief Menominee was roped and tied and hauled west of the Mississippi in a wagon, together with hundreds of his people, away from the lands of the Great Lakes which they loved. He described the spring celebration on the top of Mount Baldhead, and talked about those among their people who fled across the St. Clair River to Port Sarnia and were welcomed onto the Chippewa Reserve.

May closed her eyes a second time and was transported back to Pokagon's lodge. She could almost feel the presence of the Indian chiefs. She thought she could smell the tobacco smoke from the pipe passed around the circle of the Council fire.

"Before I sit down," Lee said, still in a quiet voice, "I want to tell you that the wilderness, as the white man called it, was not the enemy of the Indians in the old times, but a bountiful garden to be harvested with care. It has always been important to my people to think reverently about nature and to treat the animals, the people, and especially the trees and the lakes with respect. Singapore was buried because the forests were destroyed. Many Indians and many whites have forgotten this. But there is a way to remember. For *if we destroy the earth, we destroy ourselves,* because we are one with the earth which the Great Spirit created."

Lee handed the microphone to May.

She was surprised but not afraid for it still seemed as though Chief Pokagon was at her side, and she could see Aunt Nell and Uncle Steve beaming at her.

"I have been coming to Singing Sands Beach every summer since my Uncle Steve and Aunt Nell, who run the Appleby Nursery, adopted me when I was a baby in Sarnia, Ontario." May spoke clearly through the microphone. "I love the beach and the huge waters of the Lake and the Nursery where we grow flowers and trees for all of you to plant." She smiled at the audience and she felt that most of them responded kindly to her.

"This summer I discovered that I am a Potawatomi Indian like Lee. My ancestors lived here when the pine trees were so tall you could hardly see to the top of them." May paused, remembering how the virgin forests really *had* looked. "I am proud that my people had reverence for the earth and everything that grew on it." She looked directly at the people in front of her. "I want to help take care of the earth on our beach and in the Lake and I want to sign my name to be a member of the Environmentalists. I don't think we should call it *Young* Environmentalists. We should include everybody." She gave the microphone to the young president.

He shook hands with both Lee and May and

announced that those who wanted to sign the membership list should come to the front of the room.

A surprisingly long line began to form near the platform although some people shuffled noisily out the door.

"Indians," a loud male voice scoffed. "Who remembers any of them around here?"

Then May saw the little man who walked with the snake-like cane signing the registration book. She was pleased and smiled at him. He smiled back.

Aunt Nell and Uncle Steve pushed their way through the line and joined May. Tears ran down Aunt Nell's cheeks and she yanked the bandana from Lee's pocket and wiped her eyes.

"That's the way I feel about the Lake and the trees," she said. "I just never could say it."

May looked at her lovingly. Her Indian mother, May thought, had known what she was doing when she left her with the Applebys.

"Aunt Nell and Uncle Steve," she said, "I found out from Lee that I am a Potawatomi Indian and he thinks I was probably born on the Sarnia Chippewa Reserve, where he was born."

"Well, Princess, for what it's worth that's what we always kind of guessed." Uncle Steve smiled broadly.

May walked to the membership registration table with both of them and in firm letters wrote — May Apple Appleby. Then she joined Lee who was talking earnestly to the gangly young president with the unruly black hair whose name was John Sheridan. Lee caught May's hand and held it while he introduced her.

"There are a lot of problems and a lot of work and we need your help, May and Lee," John said. "If everyone co-operates the Lake might be clean enough for swimming and fishing next summer. In terms of a slogan for the campaign, though,'' and a pleased look flashed over John Sheridan's face, ''I'd really like to use what you said, Lee. That bit about *if we destroy the earth, we destroy ourselves!* In fact, it should be included in an international conservationist pledge.''

That evening May and Lee sat together on the steps of the Appleby Nursery after Uncle Steve and Aunt Nell had gone to bed. They talked about Singapore and Chief Pokagon's village and White Gull and how pleased both of them would be to know that their message would be taken up in such a special way.

''I want to go back with you, May, at the end of the summer and live on the Sarnia Reserve again,'' Lee said slowly. ''After listening to that fellow, John, I've decided I have to finish high school and then go to a university. I have to know a lot about the environment. It's really complicated today.''

The stench from the Lake mingled with the warm spring night breeze. The pollution no longer seemed like a hopeless enemy.

May and Lee looked up at the stars that sparkled clean and bright in the vast sky.

Lee took May's hand.

''You know, for the first time in my life I feel good about being an Indian,'' he said.

May smiled. ''I do too.''

Notes

1. The song on p. 54, called "The Lumberman's Alphabet", is taken from *Songs of the Sailor and Lumberman,* edited by William Doerflinger (rev. ed.), (New York: The Macmillan Company, 1972), p. 207.

2. The song on p. 56 is called "Harry Dune" and is taken from *Songs of the Sailor and Lumberman,* p. 222.

3. One incident on p. 58 is taken from Willis F. Dunbar's *Michigan — A History of the Wolverine State,* (Grand Rapids: Eerdmans Pub. Co., 1970), p. 477.

4. The quotation on p. 120 comes from *America's Fascinating Indian Heritage,* (Pleasantville, N.Y. and Montreal: Reader's Digest Association, 1978).

158

Bibliography

Ashabranner, Brent. *To Live in Two Worlds — American Indian Youth Today.* New York: Dodd, Mead & Co., 1985.

Clifton, James A. *A Place of Refuge for All Time — Migration of the American Potawatomi into Upper Canada 1830 to 1850.* Canada Ethnology Service, paper no. 26. Ottawa: National Museum of Canada, 1975.

Doerflinger, William N., compiler. *Songs of the Sailor and Lumberman,* rev. ed. New York: The Macmillan Co., 1972.

Dunbar, Willis Frederick. *Michigan, A History of the Wolverine State,* 2nd ed. Grand Rapids, Michigan: Eerdmans Pub. Co., 1970.

Hulst, Cornelia Steketee. *Indian Sketches.* New York: Longman, 1912.

Krotz, Larry. *Urban Indians — The Strangers in Canada's Cities.* Edmonton, Alberta: Hurtig Pub. Ltd., 1984.

Kubiak, William J. *Great Lakes Indians.* Grand Rapids, Michigan: Baker Book House, 1970.

Lane, Kit. *Singapore, The Buried City.* Saugatuck, Michigan: The Commercial Record, 1975.

Lenski, Lois. *Indian Captive.* New York: J.B. Lippincott, 1941.

Lorenz, Charles I. *The Early History of Saugatuck, Michigan, Its People and Sawmills.* Hamilton, Michigan, 1983.

Plain, Aylmer N. "In Retrospect," mimeo. by the grandson of Nicholas Plain Sr., the last hereditary chief of the Chippewas of Sarnia, Ontario, 1971.

Plain, Delina. "Sarnia Indian Reserve." mimeo. Sarnia, Ontario, 1979.

Plain, Nicholas. "The History of the Chippewas of Sarnia and the History of the Sarnia Reserve." mimeo. Ottawa: Dept. of Indian Affairs Library, n.d.

Project Lakewell. Bi-monthly *Newsletter,* vol. 4, no. 1. Holland, Michigan, 1981.

Schoolcraft, Henry R. *History of the Indian Tribes of the U.S.* Philadelphia: J.B. Lippincott & Co., 1857.

Sheridan, James E. *Saugatuck Through the Years 1830 - 1980.* Detroit, Michigan: Harlo, 1982.

Siegel, Beatrice. *Indians of the Woodlands.* New York: Walker, 1972.

Stone, Nancy. *The Wooden River.* Grand Rapids, Michigan: Eerdmans Pub. Co., 1973.

Tunis, Edwin. *Indians,* rev. ed. New York: Thomas Crowell, 1979.

Twitchell, Paul. *Herbs — The Magic Healers.* Menlo Park, California: IWP Pub., 1971.

Wiebe, Menno. ''Mennonites and Native People of Canada: An Intersection of Two People.'' mimeo. Winnipeg, Manitoba, 1981.

Winger, Otho. *The Potawatomi Indians.* Elgin, Illinois: The Elgin Press, 1939.

DAYS OF TERROR

by Barbara Smucker

Days of peace turn to days of terror for a young boy caught in the tensions of revolutionary times.

Set in 1917 and the years following, seen through the eyes of 10-year-old Peter Neufeld, Barbara Smucker vividly recounts the epic story of the mass exodus of Mennonites to Canada and the United States away from the horrors of anarchy, famine and the Russian revolution. Full of the joys and pains of life, *Days of Terror* is a heartrending tale recreating a dramatic period of history with vigour and authenticity.

Winner of the Canada Council Children's Literary Award
and the
Ruth Schwartz Foundation Award

"As in *Underground to Canada*, Smucker's characters manage to put the heart back into history."   — *Maclean's Magazine*

UNDERGROUND TO CANADA

by Barbara Smucker

There was bad news on the Hensen plantation. Old John brought it. "A slave trader from the deep South is comin'," he said, and fear ran trembling up and down the rows of cotton pickers, for they knew how in the deep South even tiny children were made to work in the fields with hoes bigger than themselves, and whipped for not keeping up with their work.

Julilly heard it too, chopping cotton in the blistering sun, and when lunch time came she ran to tell her mother. "Oh Lord, we is needin' your protection now," said Mammy Sally, and when night time came she whispered secretly, "There's a place the slaves been whisperin' around called Canada. The law don't allow no slavery there. They say you follow the North Star, and when you step onto this land you are free. Don't forget that place."

Next morning the slave trader came, and took Julilly away from her mother. Every day that she spent huddled in the cart in the scorching sun, travelling south or working on the brutal new plantation where the slaves were starved as thin as shadows, Julilly thought about the land where it was possible to be free, which she and her friend Liza, too, might reach some day like heaven. So when workers of the 'underground railway' offered to help them they were ready, though the slave catchers and their dogs would soon be after them.

"Barbara Smucker's book is remarkable for its fine characterization and its insightful narrative; there isn't a false note... All children should read it."   — *New York Times*

AMISH ADVENTURE

by Barbara Smucker

"Watch out!" Ian yelled.

The car wheels screamed with skidding. Suddenly the front bumper thudded into something large and brown directly in front of the car. Ian cringed. The impact jarred him and his bones felt shaken from their sockets. The brown object seemed to ooze over the car as the hood of the Volkswagen crumpled towards the windshield.

"We've hit a horse!" Jack Turner's voice was thin and reedy. "It's a horse and buggy!"

Jack Turner's reckless driving that cold, wet night was to have eventful consequences for Ian McDonald. It brought him into contact with the Amish — a gentle, peaceful folk who preferred to farm their land the traditional way — and made him realize the dangers and difficulties they faced.

Staying with the Amish was fun, far more fun than staying with stuffy old Aunt Clem, and Ian couldn't understand why everybody seemed to be so anxious to get him away from them. So when disastrous news came for the Amish farmers, Ian was even more determined to stay — but his own family had other plans....

An exciting and moving adventure, with some humorous touches, which raises questions about several things, including our often unthinking acceptance of modern values and way of life.